Jack Kerouac's Avatar Angel

His Last Novel

ALSO BY CHUCK ROSENTHAL

Loop's Progress
Adventures in Life and Deaf
Loop's End
Elena of the Stars

JACK KEROUAC'S AVATAR ANGEL

His Last Novel

with Chuck Rosenthal

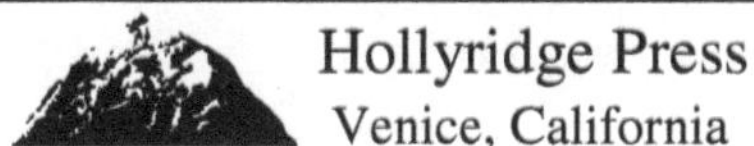

Hollyridge Press
Venice, California

 Published in the United States by Hollyridge Press.

Hollyridge Press
P.O. Box 2872
Venice, California 90294

Cover Design and Drawing by Thomas Micchelli
Author photo by Robbin Ladd
Manufactured in the United States of America by Lightning Source

Publisher's Cataloging-in-Publication
(Provided by Quality Books, Inc.)

Rosenthal, Chuck, 1951-
Jack Kerouac's avatar angel : his last novel / with Chuck Rosenthal.-- 1st ed.
p. cm.
LCCN 2001086296
ISBN 0-9676003-2-4

1. Kerouac, Jack, 1922-1969--Fiction. 2. Beat generation--Fiction. 3. Bohemianism--Fiction. I. Title.

PS3568.O8368J33 2001 813'.54
QBI21-105

First American Edition

10 09 08 07 06 05 04 03 02 01 10 9 8 7 6 5 4 3 2 1

For William Burroughs, Carolyn Cassady, Neal Cassady, Gregory Corso, Lawrence Ferlinghetti, Allen Ginsberg, John Clellan Holmes, Joyce Johnson, Jan Kerouac, Stella Kerouac, Michael McClure, Edie Parker, Gary Snyder, and Jack Kerouac.

I want to thank Gail Wronsky for her continued inspiration. I want to thank, as well, Ian Randall Wilson, Denise Stevens, and Ron Alexander for their immeasurable help with the preparation and editing of this book.

Portions of this manuscript have appeared in *Western Humanities Review* under the title "Duluoz Incarnate."

Research in Lowell, Massachusetts was funded by a grant from Loyola Marymount University.

Jack Kerouac's Avatar Angel

Introduction

I liked the Beats okay. Like a lot of kids I cut my literary teeth on Jack Kerouac and over the years had pretty much read all of him. Off and on he was the only writer I cared anything about. So when I was in New York ten years ago and found myself with a few days with nothing to do, I drove up to Lowell, Massachusetts where he was born, and where he died, too. It reminded me of my hometown, cold, overcast, wet, almost spooky.

Downtown Lowell has a monument to Kerouac, a small brick-laid park next to an old mill canal that runs off the Merrimack River. There were vertical, black marble slabs erected like a small maze, each one engraved with a quote from one of his books. It's quite a testament, really, of a town for a writer, especially one who embraced them, like he did everything else, with such profound ambivalence. Though Lowell embraced Kerouac that way, too.

I did everything backwards. First I went to the Lowell historical museum, constructed inside one of the old clothing mills. Lowell was one of the original industrial revolution boomtowns in the States and thousands of French Canadians migrated there to work. That's when Kerouac's ancestors came down, though his father ran a printing shop and his mother worked in a shoe factory. There were a lot of photographs about the mills in the museum, but at the information booth you could get a map of Lowell which included directions to Kerouac's grave and the addresses of six of the nine places he once lived.

"What about the other three?" I asked the attendant.

"I don't know," the kid said.

I stood at his grave in the rain. There were no copies of *On the Road* there, no empty whiskey bottles, no used Benzedrine inhalers, just an unobtrusive, flat stone.

John L. Kerouac— "Ti Jean"— Mar. 12, 1922 - Oct. 21, 1969—He Honored Life.

From the cemetery I followed the road back into Lowell and found Lowell high school, then Kerouac's grade school and church, St. Luis de France, where they buried his child-brother, Gerard. Back then the Kerouacs lived right across the street. From photographs I recognized his pastor, Fr. Spike, walking the sidewalk from the church to the rectory. I went to the Astro, the bar Kerouac hung out in before he died—his parents once had an apartment upstairs when it was called the Textile Lunch—I crossed the river on the Moody Street Bridge where *Dr. Sax* was spawned, then visited as many of Kerouac's homes as I could find in Centralville and Pawtucketville, the French Canadian sections. In fact, I think I found them all. Finally I ended up at 9 Lupine Road, the place where he was born.

The rain had become a drizzle and I stood there in the middle of the street in front of a two-and-a-half story house that contained at least two flats; there were full porches in front of the ground and second floors, though the top porch was propped up on tall two-by-fours. The bottom flat had gray clapboard and white trim, but the top, where Kerouac had lived, was covered by dilapidated, pale green shingles, the doors and windows trimmed in fading yellow. If the place was in repair, it was in faster disrepair. A short metal fence surrounded the place, a motorcycle with a dirty white faring parked inside, a small, dented pick-up with a camper parked in front. I couldn't help but feel a little surprised. Downtown, a marble monument, and here the place of his birth lay in ruins.

I'd never done this kind of thing before. Hadn't seen Shakespeare's grave or anybody else's. Didn't really care about the biographies of writers. I don't even like writers as people that much. In fact this quest was kind of odd in itself because I was pretty much through with Kerouac, too. There wasn't anything more I wanted to know about him, nothing of his I wanted to reread.

It began to rain again, a gentle, sad, moody rain when a little girl came down the street toward me on a bicycle, one of those old ones with the banana seat and high handlebars. She stopped next to me. She looked about seven or eight and had mud on her hands and cheeks. She wore a shabby, winter coat, open, sneakers and jeans.

Hazel-eyed, her brown hair fell to her shoulders in wet ringlets. She looked at me, then looked at the house, then looked at me again.

"Hello," she said in Quebecois French. "Good morning." It was as if she figured I wouldn't be there if I didn't speak it and, by coincidence, she was right. I was brought up only twenty miles from Canada. Though I was shocked to hear it. You wouldn't find children speaking German or Polish in either of my parents' old ghettoes.

"Hello," I said.

"Why are you here?" she asked me.

I smiled at her. "An important person was born there," I said, pointing to the second floor flat.

"Yes," she laughed. "Me."

I laughed too. "Also a famous writer, a long time ago," I said.

"In my house?"

"Yes."

"No one knows," she said.

"Well," I smiled. "That's okay." I touched her on the shoulder. "Who are you?"

"Jeanne Louise," she said.

"It was nice to meet you, Jeanne Louise," I said. "I hope it stops raining soon. I hope you have a good day and a good life."

I turned to leave but she said, "Wait. Wait. I remember something." Her features twisted in thought. "Something," she said.

"What?"

"Come with me," she said.

"I have to get going."

"Come with me, please. I'll show you something."

"Really, I don't think so," I said.

"It's right here."

"What is it?"

"I don't know just yet," she said, beginning to bicycle toward the fence. "For just a moment. Come on."

It was still early in the day, so I followed her through the gate to the back of the house. A dog barked upstairs.

"It's okay, that's just Rudy," she said. "No one is home."

She opened some double trap doors there behind the house, those kind the old places have that lead to potato cellars in the basement. I followed her down the cement stairs where she opened a cellar door. It was dark and I didn't follow her in, though she looked back at me and pointed up, at the ceiling, where a naked bulb hung from a wooden beam, a pull chain attached. I stepped in and pulled on the light.

Jeanne Louise looked around as if the place were as new to her as it was for me. She took a step, then stepped back, then stepped forward again, finally walking forward and hanging a right in front of an old gas furnace. "Come on," I finally heard. "Here." And tentatively I followed, finding her in front of a wooden chest. It looked like something that had been built by hand, hammered together from one-by-fours and painted a dark green. It had a silver latch where you'd place a padlock, but there was no lock there. The girl pulled the latch and lifted the lid. Inside was a thick roll of paper. That's all. Jeanne Louise looked rather baffled.

"Well," I said.

She scratched her head. "Yes," she said. "Well enough." She reached inside and pulled at the lip of the roll. Now, though the light was dim, I made out some print and stooped down with Jeanne Louise to look at it. Elite typewriter lettering. It had been produced by one of those big, manual Underwoods. I recognized it because my mother had an Underwood like that. We unrolled the sheet some more and I saw that the thing was apparently covered with print.

"Whose is this?" I said.

"I don't know," said Jeanne Louise. "Mine?"

"You did this?"

"Maybe," she said. "Maybe last time."

Little Jeanne Louise looked as mystified as me, though as I knelt there I had the same feeling that I got when I'd come around a bend and a car was barreling down my side of the road. I read a little of the manuscript. It had a remarkable resemblance to the style of Jack Kerouac, but I didn't recognize it as from anything else I'd ever read. I looked up and Jeanne Louise was standing now.

"From the last time I came back," she said. "The time before now."

"Came back from where?"

"From where everyone comes back from, I suppose." She knelt down again and picked up the roll and put it in my hands. "You take it," she said.

"It's not mine."

"Yes, it is." Then she turned and left.

Uncertain, I hesitated, then shut the trunk and followed her out. When I didn't find her in the yard I walked out front, and when I didn't find her there I knocked at the door to the upstairs flat. The dog barked. A neighbor watched me from a window. After a while, I took the roll of paper, walked to my rent-a-car and drove back to New York. That night I read the manuscript that is in front of you now. At the end somebody had signed it, Jack Kerouac.

I transcribed and edited the work on disc. It's about a trip Jack Kerouac took across the United States in 1982, thirteen years after his death. As in his other books, this story used pseudonyms that could be matched pretty precisely to a number of characters from Kerouac's life, many of them Beats, and I took the time to mail chapters to a number of these people as well as talk to a few of them when I could. In the manuscript here I've placed their responses after the respective sections about each of them. Some of them were written and some recorded. A good number of them, Ginsberg, Holmes, Burroughs, Jan Kerouac, are now dead.

I'm sure you have a thousand doubts and questions. So do I. But why ask them for you. I'm sure you'll ask them yourself.

Chuck Rosenthal
Los Angeles, California
January 2001

1

I am looking out over the dreamy landscape of Mexico with its poor hopeful stretching sun in the west and beyond, the brown desert stretching from here to everywhere, to the deserts of America—Texas, New Mexico, Arizona, California—to the Gobi desert and the Sahara, on the edge of which I once sat with Bull and Irwin and stared across the desert of sea, the Atlantic Ocean, and watched the sun heading for America, thinking about the Void, and the void between passages, and the passage of time, and the passage of immigrants, and the sons and suns of immigrants crossing the ocean and back again (even when you stop you're moving). It all makes me think of the gray sad east (because this is a story about going backwards). It makes me want to stop the bus and sit in the sand beside the road and roast some hot dogs over an open fire and wait for other ghosts to come by, to sit in the desert and wait for ghosts, like the Indians, who actually see them (in their peyotl dreams of ghosts who hold this ghostly world upon their shoulders, standing on Time, standing on turtles and more turtles). Maybe Cody will come by.

This is the bus back from death. The old man next to me with stubble silver beard on chin like light around the moon during an eclipse, a stubble that has been waiting for him to grow into it with enough age and wisdom and speechlessness, he has a key chain with only one key, Our Lady of Guadalupe and the flag of Mexico on little plastic holder, he, having a nap, napping in the face of end of day with the sun on his whiskers of eternity, and he is on the same bus and moving in the opposite direction (!), and who is he to care with his face napping in the verge of night, breathing the sacrament of the moment in his sleep (the sacrament of the moment, as the Jesuits say, wrong about so many things you'd have to believe they could be nothing but holy).

This is how paths cross, Gnostics, Jesuits and Buddhists, bums of Saint Teresa, old Indians with Our Lady of Guadalupe key chains and one key, and writers coming back from the dead—who would ever have to make anything up when this is the world and all you have to do is write it down! it's so simple, it's so close to heart and hand that all the great writers of the universe (and America and Europe too) have wracked their brains against the ceiling of heaven, thinking there was heaven up there, trying to *create*, (when in front of them saints are breathing out their lives in heroic breaths, working in factories and planting fields, holding babies in their bellies who are as pure and doomed as the deepest felon in Fellaheen night)—(how can anything be more sad and ironic).

In Juarez I walk the bridge to El Paso and look back across to Mexico, shacks stacked up the cliffs along the Rio Grande, in between the shacks, old American pick-up trucks (almost like the Indian reservations in Arizona and New Mexico but for the trucks being newer and the shacks more spread out there, little brick ovens and outdoor pits with black iron skillets atop, frying Indian fry bread), in these Mexican shacks women pat tortillas as white as clouds, kids running everywhere playing games with their feet, football, which we call soccer in America (unlike All-American American boys, even French Canuck ones like myself, who learned to play ball with hands, batting balls with sticks, sticking balls in hoops and running them across fields, big dreams of dribbling and batting and touching down touchdowns in the middle of America under camera lens, old men bending beer cans in their faces in that kaleidoscope of TV, dreaming their own dreams of the days they dreamed of being the big sports stars of America, probably dreaming they *actually were* the big sports stars of America) (I say this remembering my own dreams which had of course more basis in fact), but those American dreams aren't free, they require equipment, and in Mexico it's cheaper to dream per soccer ball, though in Mexico City I see some kids now and then with balls and bats.

Behind those shacks are the American factories, black stacks and gray stacks along the river, if you weren't in the desert you might think you were in Pittsburgh (old Pittsburgh, stretching its black legs out and down the Monongahela and Allegheny and Beaver and Ohio Rivers, black factories spouting fire, and you'd drive down those green rivers through towns with names like Beaver Falls and Beaver, Aliquippa and Monaca, Washington, Union, New Brighton, Freedom, Hope; houses on the hills on the other side from the factories in the showers of soot, a valley of gray houses and factories and fire and soot, train tracks along the river sparks sparking from the wheels of trains loaded with West Virginia coal, anthracite and bituminous and coke—they've cleaned all that up now I hear, Pittsburgh sitting in the center of corroding factories like a jewel, pretending to be San Francisco, people inside her silver buildings wearing white shirts and wincing and tricking at computer screens, thinking they gave all that soot to Korea —) and Mexico! (not thinking of the poor dead cities of America with their winos and sad mothers in the sootless streets, the sons of high school football stars shooting heroine and cocaine thinking in their hearts of the New America and the new sadness of America that anyway at least it's clean). No wonder why I think of Lowell.

I hear there are all new forms of dirt only now it's invisible, by-products of the great Bomb that saved us from being taken over by the Japanese, dangerous half-lives more dangerous than a whole life, pesticides and insecticides that go from outside to inside and now side against us, their very inventors! now they side with the pests and insects. I hear this from a truck driver who picks me up at a restaurant outside the bus station in El Paso where I mistake the President of the United States for a movie on the television (and I can't go anywhere without seeing a television which I knew, even in the early days of post-war pre-electro-addicted America, would replace peoples' heads), and I remember those days after coming down from Desolation and saying, ah, the world and everything in it is just a movie and we can laugh or cry but we don't have to join up, in fact we can't though we insist we do, and I was right (again!) except for having it reversed (and technologically short-sighted)—the movie is the world and the movie is on TV and the TV is on our heads, not even any rabbit ears, everybody hooked up to the same cable getting the same information, same electrons electrifying through everybody, not even watching TV but watching through TV and nobody's in charge, everybody *is* Big Brother.

We are in the truck barreling for Las Cruces. This truck driver is a big man, big arms, big belly, big thighs, big fat lipped tight smile of placidity and road concentration—he is my age and he's still working, driving an eighteen wheeler with fire painted on the hood, Bob O'Grady, Independent Trucker on each door.

"Everything is lousy and we're all tied up in the lousiness," he says. "The air is lousy, I drive a diesel. TV is lousy, I got two of them, in the truck. The president is lousy, I voted for him."

"You could have voted for the other louse," I say.

"That's right," he says, "you understand me. Have a cigarette."

Which I wouldn't normally do anymore, seeing as you have to protect your health when you're this close to death (whether you're coming or going) (tee-hee), but when you accept a ride you accept someone's generosity and it's against karma to reject the flow, this I've come to understand with age.

"You are the Buddha who says everything is lousy," I tell him.

"Damn right. The air is lousy, the water is lousy, work is lousy, the money is lousy, I sleep lousy, I breathe lousy, I eat lousy, I shit lousy. People are lousy because they don't give a lousy shit, all they care about is money. You want to watch some TV?"

He flips on a small TV on the dash and on comes a silver haired man with a big microphone interviewing a whole audience of portly ladies and everybody giving their secrets for losing weight.

"You want to lose weight you eat less," says the Buddha who says everything is lousy. "No tricks. People are idiots but you have to love them because there ain't nobody else."

And I see in that moment how this cab is wonderful in its lousiness, its digital meters metering, its dashboard lighting our faces as we cut through the desert with our truck full of American items made in Mexico, parts for food blenders in fact, parts for some kind of food machine I've never heard of, though I too am complicit because I've taken a ride, helping Mexicans work and starve so Americans can relax and eat—if I had the room I'd go to a store in Las Cruces and buy one for my mother, rest her soul, if she were here yet in America to have one—

"Las Cruces is a lousy town," says this driver who drives with his lousiness, pure and simple, and he drives me all the way to Boulder, Colorado.

2

Why would anyone come back from the dead? Why return from the dead to America except to come back and find that you did the right thing in dying in the first place? Should I look for Cody (who is dead already too) to see if he has come back somewhere to find out who he used to be? (find an article written about him in Esquire, says he died walking to heaven) (and who don't?) We don't choose birth, death, or reincarnation, or even this, to be a ghost, it happens to us like everything else.

3

Denver doldrums in the center of the world. At the east edge of the West. If you feel bad here you just have to go farther in, farther to further, further yourself farther in fur for winter flow, Flo, Floozie—I'd been in Denver wishing, knowing I couldn't get low enough, black enough, soulful enough—the ghost of Cody Pomeray, and you notice I do not say Neal, I say Cody, is floating through football stadiums, dodging waves of fanstands, the world has changed and why am I not surprised. I am older in Boulder.

And hence looking for a place to sleep, though it is summer and mid-day, because I am older and America is stiffer and I can't unroll my roll and lie down anywhere, under freeway overpass or river bridge, lip of train tunnel, in fact I'd prefer a hotel, thinking about a hotel as I smooth my hair over my bald spot when I hear a group of youngsters on the corner yelling "no - hope - a! no - hope - a!" to which I, alone in Boulder without a worry (except for finding a hotel, easy enough if you have money) and already planning on catching a bus back to Denver to stop in some lonely bar where workers stop after work and think about their lonely jobs and deaths of parents and think about their children at home and their wives at home and don't avoid them for a drink nearly so much to get away as to contemplate their own deaths and how they will die alone and even with their family gathered around they'll be there by themselves, their lives like all lives some memory of short past joys when all around them, the sad present and the shortening future, they see despair (and they see it true), I wonder where kids find no-hope-a so young and together on a street corner in Colorado.

"Hope dim glimmer in death eye!" I yell, knowing I have nothing to lose, being so old (to them) and even dead, I am invisible.

"Not *hope. Rope*."

"Rope? Nope," I say. "The Void eating hot dogs at ball games."

Now this group is clamoring about me. They're dressed strangely, with earrings in wrong places, various colors of hair, silver studs on leather jackets, black boots; two of them, I notice, are even girls.

"Naropa, Naropa."

"Naropa?"

"Do you know where Naropa is?"

"Is it a place to sleep?"

"Yes, yes, you can sleep anywhere this week. It's the Jack Duluoz Festival!"

"A Jack Duluoz Sleeping Festival!" I yell.

"That's right. Are you here for it?"

"Why else would anyone be here?"

"That's right!"

"We're dressed like Beatnicks."

"Not Beatnicks, Beats," I say to them, "and we wore sport shirts and chino pants."

"What do you know?"

"Don't bother us with the facts."

"Let's go!"

And off they go bopping and prattling and not resembling anything Beat or holy in any way except for vague energy and young ghostly ignorance.

4

This is the fate of the ghost, to encounter yourself everywhere (and the only one who can see you is yourself).

5

And the Naropa Institute is just a simple sad building like a little high school, very Irwin Garden, very Hindoo, everywhere you look people on verge of mantra (verge of dirge) taking too small of steps with heads too far forward, outside over the green chipped paint fire doors a banner saying JACK DULUOZ FESTIVAL, and outside on the lawn a man with head like gray plum sits amidst a veritable cloud of adoration and all he's saying is "ooosh rooosh pooosh, arrooom barrooom. Jack Duluoz was the greatest sound poet of all time," says he, sounding like any minute his voice is going to wander off without him and leave him there in that crowd with nothing to say—that's when I remember him and realize it must be Patrick McLear, little Patrick who used to wander at the edge of huge beat Beat crowds himself—he himself is a poet and learned all he knows from *me*! his poems say ish-ish like the wings of birds, in fact he begins to read them a poem of his own, lots of sounds of reeds under skylarks etc. but when he gets to the end he discovers the first page, started his own poem on the second page and didn't know it, everybody, even him, finding that profound in its backward profundity.

"Baarrooom!" he says. "Duluoz captured the sound of the ocean off Big Sur. Baarrooom!"

"That wasn't *baarrooom* he was saying," I say to McLear from the edge of his circled buddysattvas, "it was *barroom*. There was no liquor there and he was looking for the closest barroom."

There's a ripple, like the ocean off Big Sur, and it moves to me and back to McLear like a tiny rip tide, aah-rooo-slap (you write a lot of things in your life and people, even people who think they knew you, tend to drink it all in the same cup; for example, in my Lowell childhood soul mysteries I used a lot of French Canuck—back then, as a child, I was thinking in French Canuck—and in Mexico I used Spanish—narrative consciousness you see, nothing new, Joyce has been dead longer than me, tee-hee—which should explain something about that poem at the end of *Big Sur*, though it something about that poem at the end of *Big Sur*, though it won't, don't bother me I know better, I'm not dead for nothin) you can see McLear's teeth come together under his closed lips and I wonder if he's going to talk about walking across the cafeteria in high school again (to show, I think, sensitive pre-poetic youth, feeling simultaneous death bones world eye peeling away his skin) so self-conscious he can hear the bones creaking in his neck—he smiles.

"Don't let the myth obscure reality," he says softly chuckling in front of cafeteria teen-agers at his feet. "Some of us were there," big pause and breath, "and knew him."

I was never one much for lectures anyway, I fell asleep during my own, though I always woke up with something intelligent to say.

Michael McMclure

I once met a man who thought he was me, and you know, he was pretty convincing.

The poet wears a cloak. Metaphorically. And to be near the poet is to be near the power of metaphor. And invisibility. We all share the same sounds, but we don't use them the same way. For those who didn't know Jack Kerouac, hearing is a form of touch, and to touch my words, is to touch him. I think, and I know I am bold in saying this, because what we have here is someone who wants to touch the soul of the dead, that we must touch the souls of the dead through the souls of the living. The sounds of the living. Okay?

6

Inside that Institute it's frightening! People roving with lights and cameras, youth faces with puckered ears and autographed books, in front of an auditorium there's Irwin Garden, Simon Darlovsky, Raphael Urso leaving by back door with Jarvis Charltan (a little white haired professor Greek who I got drunk with once or twice near the end in Lowell at Nikko's Bar or sometimes Astro's Pizza-Sub, sad Pawtucketville gloaming near Moody Street Bridge, fourth floor apartment of Depression upstairs, across the street the Social Club where my father, Emil, worked and I lolled teen-age days when not playing football in Dracut, and down on corner the ghost home of death, you can hit the Moody Street Bridge from there with a stone, Dr. Sax lurking diamond eyed gloom of dark river and eternity underneath in cold steam of Merrimack River ice; Charltan said he knew me as a kid (and so did Sax!)), (and I'm thinking again of old Lowell, sad Lowell with smell of spring and mud, and river bridge like arms of dead man, the snake of the world snaked back below, hiding from that great bird of universe who disposes our earthly evil with sage beak, evil the universe disposes itself—but where does it go?) (ah, if only Sax were waiting outside that door for Irwin and Raphael and Simon and Charltan, dark hatted, sloop-eyed) I hear Raphael now, through the door, he's saying "ah fuck dat, you're fulla shit!"

And off to the side of the stage, under hound of journalism bright light, TV camera and microphone, hip under hand in sway of blonde, red lips painted red and cigarette, slightly sexy buck-toothed, Johnnie Palmer, Johnnie saying "only true love—ate six hot dogs—sold his love letter to servicemen—marriage annulled—regretted all my life," and what else is there to say but that women are holy and soft and doomed to love the madness of men who leave them in pursuance of wrongful quest, quixotic doomful concept though it be, for we ourselves are doomed by the freedom to leave, simply by not knowing any better, and so I linger unseen until everyone leaves and it's just me and Johnnie, me and Johnnie in dark auditorium, off stage in shadows, and me, returning to boyhood, heart filling with old cellular memory of Greenwich Village Manhattan, reach in my duffel and put on a hat.

"Let's go to a bar," says Johnnie. "You look old enough to get in," and we're off in car to Boulder and dark bar of afternoon, light coming in like snow or wind from open door, a man and woman in silhouette of sun pour, faces up from bar and pool table and pinball and new computer video games (which I've seen in Mexico City American hotels, orphan kids begging for pimps and hiding quarters that they don't spend for food but to play, for they know like God knows that the universe is play and that's why Jesus loves them) till dark calms down and they see our anonymity (which in age and death I've found blessed). This bar has dead animals, softball trophies, guns on the walls, a Western bar with Western music and men with tethered pick-up trucks waiting in the light, baseball hats and cowboy hats, black Naugahide booths and chrome bar chairs, glistening black padded bar of plastic or Formica, shining and new Western interior of flop up flop down—the Vision of the West that nothing lasts and all expands—I feel funny in my hat, snap down sport hat of old, little ear muffs stuffed inside like gills (which of course I never use), I look like I just came in from Nebraska on the back of some longbed truck, drinking corn whiskey under the stars with farm boys (which I've done a hundred times)—"Don't worry," says Johnnie, "they're not cowboys, they're skiers."

We order quarter pound hot dogs with our beer but when we get them from the bartender I see they don't come in buns but are sliced in half lengthwise on a slice of rye bread.

"This isn't a hot dog," I tell the bartender, "it's a wiener sandwich!" earning me bartender glare of life's heaviness of day work, the look of America which has lost its hot dogs in wiener sandwiches.

"When you cross the Mississippi you can't get a decent hot dog," says Johnnie. "Pizza either, for that matter."

"What happens to Italians when they cross the Mississippi?" I say.

"They forget," says Johnnie. "Everything is rubbed out like the River Lethe."

"Leave Lethe enough alone," I say, and go to juke box and plethora of country western honey drip, dipping sadly for Parker or Gillespie or even Leadbelly, something of the East, and Memory, when I spot Billy Holiday, some miracle of modern forgetfulness (or some slipping spy act of down and out Philadelphian, grease-haired, stuck by some mystery in Boulder with job filling juke boxes with country tunes, slips in one of his favorites, raises the collar of his coat, hooo-hooo ha-ha-ha, what will they think of this!), and with a quarter I play "I Cover the Waterfront" and go back to bar where Johnnie like Mephisto of old has finished her wiener sandwich and already ordered another. "It could be worse," I tell her, "it could be Grosse Point, Michigan."

"Or a fishing village without water," says Johnnie, referring, I know, to old Lowell and the day we visited the street of death. "Don't tell me, there's nothing wrong with Grosse Point for a straight, old woman."

I see the ghosts in her eyes and touch her cheek, saying with fingertip what sticks behind my lips, what suddenly I cannot say, that I am back, I am here, and again I am already gone.

"But you can really eat," I say instead, in my best Bogie, remembering days on Upper West Side, downing huge breakfasts and munching ripe olives, cold asparagus with mayonnaise.

"Another hot dog and another drink," says Johnnie—she is still blonde, still beautiful, still that beauty of the American night who braless in T-shirt smoked marijuana openly in West End Bar. "What are you doing here," she says to me, in munching aggressive hot dog bites, "with all these horrible bourgeois kids and middle-aged ex-hippies."

"Not a better question in the universe," I say to her, thinking again to myself (as I will a thousand times on this trip back to the beginning, back to emptiness, back to darkness) this is the dark I return to, this is darkness, the womb, Johnnie, my first wife. "I'm here to write about some things that I missed the first time."

"Another writer. There's so many goddamn writers. And so little ammunition."

"Schools of writers, pools of writers, colonies!"

"Nations!" shouts Johnnie. "Societies! Cultures!"

"Germ cultures! Yogurt cultures!"

"Culture vultures!"

But we are shouting too loud for cowboy skiers and drivers of small Japanese trucks and the bartender is asking us to quiet down.

"Do you know who you're talking to?" says Johnnie to tired face of bartender and wiener sandwich server under rattle of Western bar liars' dice, "I was married to Jack Duluoz!"

"And your friend," says bartender, "is he Mr. Duluoz? or you cheating on him?"

"That's true," I say.

"What's true?"

"I am related to Napoleon!" I shout. "And King Arthur too!"

"He doesn't give a shit," says Johnnie.

"Not as long as you're quiet and buy drinks," says bartender.

"I'm Rimbaud," I tell him, "and she's Baudelaire."

"Okay, Rambo."

"Rim*baud*!"

"Let's get the hell out of here," says Johnnie, "before he finds out who Rimbaud is and you find out who Rambo is."

I never find out who Rambo is. In car of fading afternoon, the sun in mountains, I wish for Cody Pomeray. Think about this. I have returned. Why not Cody? Why not the car of heaven driving to the ends of earth?

"Let's drive to Denver," I say to Johnnie. "Let's drive and drive."

"You remind me of somebody," she says. "Those sad blue eyes."

"Prince Myshkin?"

"Burl Ives."

In her motel room I forget that I am Jack Duluoz, forget that I've been gone for unmistakable lost memory dream of years. It's hot sweaty Manhattan night, we'll make love and I'll wonder how anyone still so beautiful and soft could want the hairiness and roughness of a man, could want the protuberance of manhood, the fluids of manhood, and what are the dreams of women who wish to be filled this way? what are the dreams of women? (does she dream of the months I grew inside her with my son, awakened to death before he dreamed his life in the sometime in the same night that's everywhere the same right now and forevermore? if to be alive is to dream beyond whatever we are, what are the dreams of the womb? the dead?—I will tell you now that life is the dream of the dead) what are the dreams? and afterwards we'll walk the streets—our sweat still mixing, our fluids a poetry of perfume—and look for the jazz and madness still left in America underneath the detective TV shows and deodorant and mouthwash and beer adds of American Nazi Corporatism and in the bars of night find the great subterranean writers of America, reckless, depressed, brooding the brew of unpublishable manuscript art (not knowing that editing is death, too, and they live in anonymous bliss), they want to die on the cross of recognition and who am I to tell them no?

Again Ti Jean I rest on Johnnie's woman breast in moment thirty years old. In breath of love like breath of death (the Hindus say the soul is breath) I've said these things already to her aloud. She lights a cigarette and I wish there were neon somewhere to illuminate the smoke so I can feel low down and mysterious like some cheap novel that was never my life but was somebody's life somewhere, some dream of life of a living man. I sing whisper "Frankie and Johnnie were sweethearts, glory how they could love—"

"Stop that," says Johnnie.

But now I am in Memory and glooming. There are things a man must pour from heart even if heart of ghost.

"I called you 'Frankie' sometimes. I called you Birdnote."

"Stop it."

"I cried on your steps in Grosse Point after car accident, saw Christmas wreath on your door and passed out thinking you were dead."

"I loved that man," says Johnnie. "I married him. I saw him buried."

"Your eternal old man."

"I fucked a nut," she says.

"I'm Jack."

"Jack who?"

"Duluoz. I'm back."

"Back from where? Where have you been? You can't impersonate somebody who's been dead for years."

"That's what I'm saying!"

"Jesus," she says. She's out of bed, moving into her clothes. "Anybody can read that stuff, it's everywhere."

"Just look at me."

"I don't have to look at you, I've seen plenty already."

And suddenly I am seeing the ironies of life pounding toward predictable consequence, that once years ago I left Johnnie (like it seems I have left all women, even my sweet Mémêre and last dear wife, even Tristessa who waits in Mexico in generations of sadness), and on the day of great regret of my leaving, The Jack Duluoz Festival of the Naropa No-Hope-a Institute, I return anonymous and rejected, that living or dead the last good-bye is never in present tense. It's only been thirteen years but I am wearing some mask of death (my father coughing in his death chair said his mind was still so young, the mind of youth in the mask of age and I some mind of death) in mask of life.

"This is a bad routine," says Johnnie. "It's some kind of reverse perversion."

And she asks me to leave while I remember that as we entered I noticed there wasn't even a vacancy in this same hotel! I'm stuffing old bones in pants, panting old stuff in air.

"Hot dog annulments!" I yell.

"Now you sound like Urso!" says Johnnie. She's looking for something, a weapon, but settles for high-heeled shoe. "Read something worthwhile!"

I scramble for duffel and shoes and hat as she shoves me out. "We drew the Underground Man and you painted his toes!" I yell and with this earn moment in mind of Golden Eternity at doorstoop and Johnnie lets drop hand of high heeled attack, stops to stand staring out door at me who even in summer has breath hot enough to smoke cool Boulder night.

"You're mixing me up with somebody else," she says, but they are the sad soft words of another time looking into pool of Time, and the door clicks with gentle click of recognition of regret, and Memory (so close it sounds to Mémêre who I, Ti Jean, am son and babe of both), and am wise enough now to know it was for these moments why I came back.

Edie Parker

A friend of mine who lives in North Beach now, a writer—I guess I should just say her name is Alice and leave it at that; there's already enough libel in this book and I don't need to be a part of it—though she's not a Beat writer, she's more one of those *New Yorker* writers, you know, family histories, a lot of stereotypes about the coasts, particularly Berkeley and North Beach, old houses, changing seasons, you know, fuddy-duddy stuff; Alice told me that the only reason she ever went to a writers' conference was to get laid, and she's not a young woman either.

This guy was kind of sweet. Maybe he did remind me of Jack a little. It was the Jack Kerouac Festival. We were all a little nostalgic. I'm not ashamed. It's not the first time I got laid. For Christ's sake, he used a condom.

7

I find Irwin in the phone book, why not? it's civilized America in civilized world, you can look up old Beat poets in phone books, hook up bold new phone worlds to poets pumping poems by modem into literary magazines (they all sound the same now anyways with their little epiphanies about horseback riding horse-shit or watching whales) (poor whales, you wonder what they did in own primal pasts to inherit our poisoned seas, poisoned poems, we give them our broken refrigerators, ovens, washers and dryers, oil, they don't know what to do with them, wearing no clothes themselves, having no frozen foods, no automobiles, don't have no repairwhales anyway, then they get fed up, they swim up rivers, they come ashore—we send them back! somebody should have done that to us!)—Irwin always did want to be institutionalized and his stint in the mental institution didn't de-institutionalize him, it just made him want to start an institution of his own, now he's an institution of American poetry himself, probably votes Democrat (and I remember telling him when he wrote "The Great Flower Sutra" that it was really his "O Captain, My Captain," yours truly sitting with him there along the tracks, drinking tokay and watching locomotive wind on sunflower death)—so I'm not surprised to peek in his front window on Pine Street Boulder, CO and see him at rocking chair fireside, wine in hand balanced just so-so in round bubble glass, still in his No-hope-a coat-a, tie and beads, belly bulging over suit pants (though relieved to see the bottom button of his shirt open with stomach hair poking through).

Across from Irwin is tall man in other rocking chair, silk shirt Italian shoe type, full gray hair head, chiseled faced famous American poet if you ever saw one. There's nothing for me to do but knock on the door.

"Oh humm, umm," says Irwin at the door, "do I know you."

I still have my hat on and I've got my duffel bag. I just walk in. Nice hard wood floors, Indian carpets, some kind of soft jazz on the stereo, I can see it now across from the fire, all black and very technological in one big column.

"That's a nice stereo," I tell him.

His poet friend stands up, I can see he's a little disturbed seeing as he's a special guest in anybody's house and not used to being interrupted let alone by old bums in the night (but this is a special night, this is the night when the ghost comes and you never know when he's coming, that's the part about it that's just like everything else).

"Humm," says Irwin.

"Old friend," I say, shaking the poet's hand, "dropped in out of dark, thrown out by old girl friend, world never changes."

"Martin Standoff," says famous soft hand poet.

"That Russian?"

"Canadian," says Standoff. "Born in Newfoundland." He says Newfoundland like it's the beginning of a long narrative he doesn't want to get into, being a lyric poet himself.

"Canadian myself," I say. "French."

"You don't say," says Standoff obviously put off, not knowing he is in the face of the greatest living writer back from the dead in America.

"Well, um, something to drink?" says Irwin.

"Something brown and straight up, none of that fancy grape stuff."

"I'm kind of an old friend of Irwin's, too," says Standoff.

"You don't say," I say.

"Well," says Irwin, pouring my whiskey from a decanter that looks like it belongs in the Thomas Jefferson room in the Smithsonian, "kind of friendly competitors."

"Nemesis might better describe it," says Standoff, "all for the greater love of art, of course, and Irwin's even greater disdain."

"Sixties," says Irwin, mumbling into his wine bubble. He looks like those comic book people who live under water and have to have glass water jars on their heads when they come on land. "Very political times."

"Actually, it was the early seventies," says Standoff.

"Hmm, maybe," says Irwin, "not that it matters."

"Well don't let me get in the way," I tell them. "I'll just sit here by the fire, maybe go in the kitchen and make myself a sandwich, I've never been much of a talker anyway I just like to drink and listen and remember for eternity."

You have to give things to Irwin, even though he was living like poet king in Boulder—not that I blame him, the first thing I did when I made buck from book was buy a house for me and my sweet Mom—and though he was entertaining stiff gray haired Russian-Canadian-Newfoundlandish poet and busted in on by bum of unrecognized past, me, coming to realize that in this mask of death I had become an impossible and unconscionable and consequently imperceptible self, so that even my old friends and lovers (and wives!) do not recognize the very thing they see (me! Jack Duluoz!) a percept without concept, existing and invisible at the same time, even so Irwin let me in his home for sandwich and whiskey, unquestioned.

My ghost sits by in his miraculous chair. Maybe I am not there at all. Maybe I fall asleep. Because it goes on a long time. Irwin Garden and Martin Standoff, the two great poets from the opposite ends of America are sipping wine in Irwin's house in Boulder in the middle of the Jack Duluoz Festival with the dead and returned and unrecognized Jack Duluoz, not talking about me or writing or books or even poetry. I'm dozing to talk of electro-fusion jazz, fine wines, the Denver Nuggets and the Utah Jazz! What are they? Professional basketball teams! Irwin a Nuggets fan! Standoff lives in Salt Lake City! The great American Russian Canadian Newfoundlandish poet living with the Mormons! (birthplace of Cody in all unlikelyhood, get out of bus, walk around temple right across street, see glistening face and bland eye Disney America, feel obligation to litter and get back in bus).

"Baseball," I say to Irwin. "You're a smart man. A Jewish man. A homosexual. An intellectual. Follow an American game."

"Basketball was invented in Massachusetts," Standoff reminds me.

"I know where basketball was invented! We invented the atom bomb, but we don't have to like it. It doesn't make it American. In fact that's exactly it. The Russians have basketball and the atom bomb and use them with equal lumbering domination, but they'll never be any good at baseball."

"Well hmmm we only have a farm club in Denver," says Irwin. "Hoping for a major league team."

"The same in Salt Lake," says Standoff, "they don't even warm up before games, they sleep in the outfield."

"All the better! That's what I mean. You'd never find a Russian sleeping in the outfield."

"Russians sleeping in our outfields," mumbles Irwin.

"But we have a good wine store in the center of town," says Standoff.

"In Salt Lake City?" says Irwin.

"No more talk about wine!" I yell.

"Did I get your name?" Irwin asks.

"I knew you when you wouldn't be caught dead with clothes on, Irwin, let alone this business get-up. What is this music?"

"Something quiet enough to speak over," says wine sipping Standoff. "Subtle." He looks at me like that's a word I don't know.

"You hit somebody on the head till they're numb, then that little tingling they get, that first feeling just as they're coming to—that's subtle."

"You don't say."

"I do say."

"I've toured with Bob Dylan, the Grateful Dead, The Clash," says Irwin.

"You don't say," says Standoff.

"You here for the Festival?" I ask him.

"A reading at the University. Something in the cosmos must have wanted to offset the hotbed of bad taste."

"Good taste is spineless. Tell him Irwin."

"We're here to forgive, er, permit, acknowledge and permit differences," says Irwin.

"You ever been published in the *New Yorker*, Irwin?" says I.

"Well, I'm sure you won't find Martin in City Lights," says Irwin, coming out of that wine glass for a minute for a breath of common air.

You can't hide in a wine glass, I want to tell him. The only way to hide good is to die.

"But like Martin," says Irwin, "I've read at the University of Colorado. I've read in Salt Lake. The Clash meets the *New Yorker*, so to speak. It's what America gives us in its semblance of free speech, the university, a meeting of opposites in a middle called the left, and we attempt to nudge the middle around. Did I get your name?"

"How about *The Atlantic*, Irwin. How about *Harpers*?"

"They haven't excluded me from attention."

"That little cameo about you and Simon in Benares in the July '63 *Esquire*?" 'Such sights and smells charmed the Beats'? They were interested in your *charm* so much, how about publishing a few poems?"

"We engage in ephemera while the fascists run the show," says Standoff.

"For some it's ephemera," says Irwin, "but if it is, then it's all ephemera. For me it's as real as the oppression. But it's contemporary corporate anti-soul America. You can't divide things up like you would a cheesecake."

"A rather benevolent oppression," says Standoff. "Good cheesecake, too, even if we have to import it."

"Are we talking about the same stuff?" I ask Irwin.

"Are we having a disagreement? Have you tried any of the Pinot Noir from Oregon?" says Standoff.

"I've toured with the Gang of Four, as well as The Clash," says Irwin.

"Who is that?" I ask Irwin. "A truck accident and Chinese revolutionaries? What is this touring? Do you get a touring car?"

"That's the first thing you've said I agree with," says Standoff.

"That's frightening," I tell him. "That makes me tremble."

"Would you like some more scotch?" says Irwin.

"I wouldn't've believed it the last time my mother and me chased you out," I tell Irwin, "but you were better off like that than this. Now my mother would like you. I'll have to be dead another thirteen years to straighten it out."

"Dead?" says Irwin.

"You wouldn't understand. Why do you think I'm here and not with Johnnie."

"Yes, I've been wondering about that the whole time," says Standoff poet of off-handed irony wisdom.

"You look familiar, but I can't quite place you, it's funny," Irwin says. "Did I get your name?"

"Jack."

"Jack?"

"Duluoz!" I say. "I'm Jack Duluoz!"

"You don't say," says Standoff.

"I think that's what he's saying," says Irwin.

"It's been a few years since you published anything," says Standoff.

"Because I'm dead!"

"I think I better go," says Standoff.

"No, no, I'm going," I tell him, standing up. "You were here first."

"Well, um, please," says Irwin. He has that look he never had as a young man. His eyebrows come together like he's thinking about something on a menu. "Don't go yet."

"I have to go now, I'm just doing reconnaissance."

"And you finally recognized something," says Standoff.

"That's right."

"Please stay a bit," says Irwin.

"Can't. If I do I'll turn into something horrible. Irwin, I'll turn into your mother!"

8

You come back for the last word and you don't get it, life is cruel to the living and cruel to the dead, sad on both sides.

Allen Ginsberg

I am not a Denver Nuggets fan. Professional sports is a type of corporate slavery which uses the bodies of black men, a select few of whom make a lot of money for a brief period, many more of whom are exploited by colleges and universities, the rest opiated by the glitz of the handful who get to perform for millions of Whiteys, making billions for the white corporate sex beer patriarchy, keeping millions more of the oppressed mired in the American dreamscape. If I discussed the Nuggets with Standoff (is this Mark Strand?) it was an act of conciliation. I am not always willing any-more to go to war over every word, nor does my politics leave me incapable of appreciating the poetics of the forward pass.

I'm trying to remember where Peter could have been during all this, and didn't Strand visit me in 1984? aside from that, it was the Jack Kerouac Conference, not Festival, though I wouldn't put it past Jack to intentionally confuse the terms for the sake of hyperbole.

Now, Buddha Nature blasts world sometimes coming out in persons, moments; the naive Western soul of Western conception, dialectic, personality—illusion, does not transmigrate, does not cosmically compute—people don't come back from the dead, personalities die in living beings, let alone dead ones—Kerouac never was always was—blasts of him in the sentences of the world, thirty years later, bursts in insurance salesman consciousness, crack addict, Vietnam veteran, pot smoking teen-ager, astronaut, Soviet underground rock star, priest, bum, Hollywood screenwriter—I see him everyday and I was at his funeral—my way of refusing commentary on question—did Jack Kerouac visit me in 1982? did he die in 1969?

9

Aah wreckage. Time wreckage, rhyme wreckage, five & dime wreckage, slime of time glumming its wrecked wroughtness, who else, thinks I, is dead in the Boulder night? no hope, no dope, no hope for rope of hope at home of Narop(a)—I am dead and as filled with sound as ever in my deadness (some things do not change) (others change)—why do you think I'm writing this book anyway? not to find the past lurking shadowly and gloomful beneath the past, beneath memory (I remembered good enough the first time); I've got you by your reading brain and you don't think that's good enough? how and where does a ghost get pulled? I wish I knew, but you can't know ahead of time so you write it down later, just like everybody else; but get this straight: I'm not doing this to straighten anything out—am I Duluoz back from the dead, off the road of life and sorrow? the road of death is sorrow too, don't be fooled, there's no escape, you spend some time in enforced meditation, you get more sophisticated—remember, I'm not here because I owe you anything, except, maybe, for one last sober book, sober look (not to tell you whether or who I slept with on the USS Weems, friendly merchant marines) crooking like periscope around corner of Time—do you think the biographers will tell you who Irwin Garden is? Bull Hubbard? do you think anybody knows but me? how better to answer the question? why bother?

There is still a bar open in Boulder.

And at bar stool at bar, white teeth and pink gums out of mouth and on black bar top, hunched like toad on toad stool but for black hair of mop, squat back vested, Urso, Raphael.

"Duluoz," he says. "About time. Now you tell me something. Do I look like Pete Rose?"

"Who's Pete Rose?"

"Who's Pete Rose. What, you don't get papers over there?"

"They're in Spanish."

"So it's Pedro Rosa or something, Pete Rose is Pete Rose everywhere, what do you think. Some fuckin kid comes up to me with a copy of *Howling*, he says, here, sign this, I say, sign what? what's this? he says, it's all I got, sign it, 'To Tim, Good Luck, Pete Rose.' So I did. I signed it for Irwin too, Love, Pete and Irwin. Shit. You better get a drink before this bar closes. Fuckin podunk. All these mystic types want to live in podunk. Look at Ryder, that fuckin nut, up in the hills above Grape University Writing School."

"Japhy! In riding school!"

"Where did you hear that?"

"From you!"

"Where did I hear that?"

"I don't know! I just got here!"

"You heard it here, that's where. There's been more shit floating around here than a dormitory commode. Duluoz this and Duluoz that, I shouldn't of come. They got some of the greatest living poets in America here, well, two at least, one anyway, they got 'em right here in front of them and they want to talk about a dead guy, no offense, but they got us right here in front of them; next year I could be dead, they'll be going to everybody else for information that they could of asked me right here. It's fuckin ancestor worship. They can't put you on the mantle until you're dead. Keep your fat live ass off the mantle. They want to know about the Beats. They don't know nothin about the Beats. They all read the same stuff. There's some woman here, some fuckin big shot from somewhere, writing a memoir about Duluoz and the Beats and she hardly fuckin knew us! She was a kid in New York the same time we were there. She's got a chapter about what she was doing and then a chapter about what we were doing—same stuff you read everywhere—then later she sleeps with you, Duluoz, she slept with you, like that's some special category, give me a break, that makes her an authority—not that there weren't important women, there were plenty, we both know that, but we fucked them and put them in insane asylums where *we* belonged."

"It's probably a juxtaposition of uncommons," I tell Raphael. "It's a narrative technique. Place two separate worlds side by side, except of course in a narrative prose you can't do that, you have to place them one after another, contiguously you might say, and that makes you see parallels you might not have seen if you hadn't thought about those two worlds as simultaneous before. Those worlds are represented of course by the main characters in them and when those two make love you get the opposite, you get the uniting of those worlds, the metaphor of all love, the uniting of opposites, cosmic and otherwise, only by witnessing that conjugal moment you come to realize that those worlds are irreconcilable. Your friend probably has that realization herself in her memoir right at that moment, and that's when she makes her passage from the adolescent/child world of the Beats to the real adult world of work-a-day work, sad as it is, the Beats aren't the answer. You just have to get a job and be American sad. I can tell you what that book's about and I haven't even read it. You, Urso, being a rather lyric type, can't recognize these narrative formulas which I myself abandoned before I wrote *Road*. What are we to expect? Joyce and Proust didn't change publishing."

"That's exactly what scares me about death," says Raphael, "that it's going to give me distance. So what do you do over there. Do you fuck? Do you get drunk?"

"It's a lot like Mexico. Did she say I was good in bed?"

"She's cynical for chrissake, too smart to get hooked up with a jerk like you, besides she thought you were an impotent, brooding egomaniac. But don't think that'll stop her from putting a picture of you on the cover."

"She pretty?"

"Nah, just some fat girl, probably married to a fag now. You never had any discrimination. You got plenty of people saying you were passionate and handsome, even a genius. Christ, I even said you were a genius, I told some guy with a camera and microphone yesterday you bordered on the fuckin sublime, I must of been drunk, like now."

"I didn't know this was going on," I tell Raphael. "I was heading for Denver, got truck ride here, ran into Johnnie who threw me out, found Irwin in his place drinking wine and jazz with Martin Standoff."

"You're back for forty days like Jesus. You want to trace your steps, leave everybody with little tongues of fire over their fuckin heads so they can go out and get it right this time. Cody's dead, dusted, he was dusted before you were. I need another drink."

It's last call in Boulder bar and again I am drinking in America, thinking it's America that makes me drunk, America with its dark sad bars for escaping sadness—nothing changes but the threat of death—A Bomb, planet bomb bomb blast bombast—men still cheat on women in hotel rooms, supply closets, college professor offices, come to bars to mull it out, who do I love more? what do I love to lose? (lose to booze), making misery of life, wife's life, kid's life, mistress's life, all for desire, for to come here to these dark places is to desire something else (peace and death) (and that comes all too soon not soon enough); and there's the mortgage and the car and insurance and bills and the kid's school (can't send 'em to public school, they learn nothing there, better to be slapped alphabetically by nuns)—it's enough to walk the streets of any American town and see the dim house lights by shade in night, the screen of color TV blaring hamburger magic of next pool, next car, one thing leads to another so the poets get drunk for them all, get drunk for America so the rest can get up and go to work.

"Let's get out of here," I say to Raphael.

"I thought you were as out as you could get. Now you're back."

"Let's go to Denver."

"I ain't going to Denver."

"Anywhere! Take me away from the Jack Duluoz Festival!"

"Okay, I'll take you to the deadest place on earth. Deader than Death Valley. Deader than a fuckin cemetery. Deader than anyplace they speak Spanish."

And we are off in Naropa Institute borrowed van, crossing Rocky Mountains in splaying dawn light of breathtake mountain shadow glacier gray spread of granite height, weaving on winding rock roads, weaving in new wakefulness; Raphael, teeth on dash next to steaming Styrofoam coffee cup, hands over wheel like cathedral gnome in church of Rocky Mountain sky steeple, brow over eye,

eye over highway, lipstuck, silent. Where do you go when the dead come to you, blood beating in cheek? Is this what happens to poets in late age? he wonders under dark hair (for returned from death or no I know these things, not confined to limited prescience of writer memory, or even narrative stratagem hatagem of old voice, old books—methinks the thoughts of all things tarrying on page, characters and otherwise; youthinks I have not read me Tolstoy?—), every poet should travel in van on Rocky Mountain road with dead King of Beats, why not? (last words I spoke to Stevarino Allen on New York night street, he wondering why I drank so much and me not willing to flap lip one more time about Catholic Baptism, curse of holiness; why not, Stevarino? yelling at end of block so he wouldn't have time to answer back, advantage also of the page and even better when dead and don't have to read reviews, tee-hee).

"So who else you seen?" says Raphael.

"I saw Simon leave the stage with you and Irwin and Charlton, and I saw McLear on the lawn outside the Insta-toot."

"But you only talked to Johnnie and Irwin."

"McLear for a minute but he was too busy telling everybody about me."

"And nobody recognized you."

"Not yet. Maybe later."

"Well you can't blame them. You look a lot better than just before you died, and people have a lot invested in your death, you got to understand that. They were at the funeral. They got empirical evidence. Notice what I'm talkin about. Facts. If you studied anything besides that Romantic bullshit you'd have some idea."

"I didn't come with an itinerary."

"You got to know about science, better, technology. You hear what I'm sayin? Comte was right but Huxley was righter, and then you got to think about McLuhan and Marcuse. They took the tops off all the crosses, put naked girls on 'em, put 'em in orbit and made them satellite TV antennas. That's what happened since you been gone."

"I died a few years ago."

"You died a fuckin long time ago. Thirteen fuckin years ago you died."

"It's not the kind of thing you control," I am telling Raphael as we slide down side of mountains, white box bobsled van zooming carooming, Raphael twisting over wheel like wrestler crunching head; "it's not vacation. No hotel reservations, no plane train tickets, rent-a-cars, phone calls to friends to see if you can stay overnight, no pack up wife kids in station wagon; it's *impromptu*!"

"Station wagons went out when you did. They all drive mini-vans now, recreational vehicles and other multi-syllabic euphemisms for distraction!"

"From death!"

"Yes!"

"From the multi-faces of Buddha's joy!"

"Which is Death! From freeway airjet microwave!"

"Death, too! From God!"

"Also death! From God's dogs at heels!"

"From dead/Beat poet kings!"

But not from IT. This is not Cody and this is not long ago. And is this even Raphael who I remember young and silent, brooding, over great Dostoyevskian existence depression—this no fruit cart ride—no New York/San Francisco—no Mardou—no illusion—no God thought stopped thinking—some Time moment not time (like Buddha thought of all thought)—not the IT—not ever IT—to think, that Cody was wrong—that there really is a past?

Out of mountains into Colorado high desert, heading for Utah on *freeways* stripping stripes (have you seen a map?) across America, avenues, corridors of boredom, no hitch-hiking (unless you're some kind of crazy hoodlum bent on death or someone's death with someone wanting to die to pick you up, no time to stop anyway, cars whooshing, signs everywhere say you must be some kind of motorized vehicle for access to, whoosh), no wending or winding, no towns, no billboards, no mountain pass, no stop signs, no stopping at all, just asphalt tubing in tin can like pneumatic messages *au Paris*, no barn relics, red brick churches, graveyards, schoolhouse, if you want gasoline must exit off long deceleration ramp to island of plastic and lights, ask gas station attendant (after you fill up yourself, wipe own windshields, pay ahead of time) "is this Vermont or Kansas?" probably won't know, have to turn on TV to find out.

Across bleeding southern Utah canyon Mars, I-70 to I-15 (actually a little portion in between connection where not on freeway where cars come from other direction and have to stay on own side of road except to pass, but now it's Utah and it doesn't matter), down to desert, shoot through Virgin River Canyon Arizona and out other side to Nevada Yucca trees, enough sun for a million things, Raphael parks van at roadside (illegal now of course in modern road law America, stopping and going being completely separate activities which must be regulated with tremendous care lest one think one was necessary to the other) and we tromp into desert to wait for lizard pie sunset for no special reason but as to not hit Las Vegas before dark and miss lights of city as we drive in from fifty miles away—like Zen monks eating beef—but it's only Las Vegas, even lit up, hardly dead to depths of death, brain dead heart dead greed dead deed dead do-da daylight electric potbellied sportshirted hope of doubling money, at least everybody understands they're really there to lose, enough cheap metaphors of life for any story—jewel of sadness and wealth, loss and profit in American desert culture, Hoover damn hooving and behooving its Colorado River power light (always reminding me of Hoover vacuum cleaner owned by Mémêre, sloping fenders like 1930's Chevrolet, headlight lighting way to bold future of floor sweeping when robots do all, should have had angels on wings like damn, zodiac signs on plastic swooping hood, time when America thought all was monument and some future race would find our vacuum cleaners and damns and think us pretty neat (hee-hee!)), probably why so many TV shows set there—but we won't see Hoover Damn because we are coming from other direction. I tell all this to Raphael.

"Vegas ain't dead Mecca, it's just limbo," says Raphael. "We're just going to rest here."

We drive down strip. Lit lights neon golden Aladdin's, Sahara, MGM, Pioneer, Raphael rolling van into Oriental Palace (across from Caesar's) where he says we can room for $18/night, goes off to slot machines while I wait in line for room till I reach young late-teen-age girl clerk, eyes dull as poker chips, straight blonde hair at shoulder and smile of addict wishing for dime (a smile of the unnamed blankness filled with want)—"Duluoz," she says, "I had to read a book by a Jack Duluoz for school."

"Did you like it?"

"Did you write it?"

"What title?"

"*Road*, I think. I didn't finish it. I thought, you know, those people were wasting their lives, they didn't care about anything but drugs."

"And sex and cars," says I. "What do you care about?"

"Oh, you know, money. Maybe I'll have some kids someday. Did you write anything else?"

"No, after that I lost my mind and drank myself to death."

"That's too bad. Maybe you should have stayed at it and written something really moving someday."

I'm saved by Raphael who's won $75 on the quarter slots.

"It means nothing to me," he says, "that's why I win. Being dead, you'd probably clean up."

"You won money, let's go see Sinatra at Caesar's Palace."

"I don't want to see him, he turned into a fat old crook."

But everybody's a crook in America, everybody who makes a dollar or spends a dollar or turns on a light is stealing the life of the world, buying a dollar of atomic chemical half-life half-death, horrible crookedness horror horror, and why be a sappy baby about it, renting an $18 room in the Oriental Palace, heading for some Deadland in land of living in stolen Naropa van and not go see Sinatra?

"Yeah, but somewhere you got to draw a fuckin line," says Raphael who does not draw the line and we throw our bags in room and head for Caesar's Palace where Sinatra is SOLD OUT. Been sold out for weeks. Years, Raphael says. We cross street and circle around corner and eat at Italian restaurant, all the cheap Dago red you can drink if you buy a plate of spaghetti for $10 and I tell waitress (dark horsy girl but petite, too, like one of those Arabian horses somebody'd keep on a farm in Oxnard) that for $10 I should be able to buy spaghetti and Dago red for whole restaurant.

"Hey, fantastico! You having the spaghetti?"

"He sure is, and me too," says Raphael.

All around on walls are autographed photographs, movie stars, John Wayne, Bing Crosby, Frank Sinatra, right underneath basket wrapped Chianti bottles and fake grapes.

"I'll give you my autograph," I tell her.

"Fantastico! Who are you?"

"Jack Duluoz."

"He's back from the fuckin dead," says Raphael.

"Fantastico! But we got some dead people up on the walls already."

"But you took those pictures before they were dead."

"What's the difference?"

Good question, only proving that even in the cranium of petite horsy chicks working cheap in Vegas lurks sense of death born from and returned to, first and last womb.

"And this is Raphael Urso, famous Italian Beat poet who's had his picture taken with Death many times over, even going to his birthday party and writing a book about it."

"You speak Italian pretty good," Raphael tells her.

"You having spaghetti?" she says.

"Yeah, I said yeah already."

"Fantastico! We'll take your picture. You can sign it. The owner will decide if he wants to hang it up."

A man comes in with an accordion and sings "That's Amore!" He asks us where we're from.

"New York," says Raphael.

"Hey, I been there, that's in New York State. Where you from?" he says to me.

"Heaven."

"You're in heaven right now."

"That's right."

And in comes photographer with big old fashioned fat camera like the days when cameras were important and pictures were important and something had to be important to make it worth your while—fat lensed, huge tubed, flash bulb sitting on top a tower with aluminum reflector disc, flash of light ignites room—he has that photo developed and printed before we get done eating and Raphael and I sign it right there at the table on the red and white checked table cloth, Jack Duluoz and Raphael Urso, date it 1982, which is a document, of sorts, of my return, though you'd have to find the restaurant and search the walls, or find the owner if he didn't bother to put the picture up there next to all those movie stars and fake grapes, and ask him to see that picture if he hasn't thrown it away, and even if you did, who would you think you were believing your own eyes anyway?

10

Did I say I was going to write a *different* book? It's just a story of the world and what happened in it. You want a different version read somebody else. You want somebody else's story of Jack Duluoz (God bless 'em), go read 'em. Write your own (who's stopping you?).

11

The Land of the Dead is Disneyland.

12

It's not the old Disneyland that you watched on black & white TV at 5 o'clock on Sunday nights. Even if you were in your thirties (like me) you knew that all over America it was growing dark and beginning to snow (again) and kids everywhere were huddled next to steam radiators with hot chocolate and blankets and pajama-ready bed and tomorrow and school already lurking in dark long week ahead (and is Sr. Mary Helene going to slap my knuckles for homework forgotten, catechism question falling short in trip from brain to tongue—heart got in the way and made me play in snow—for tree colored blue instead of green—at time felt so good about that tree—but let's forget about it and watch Disney where he takes you to a place in Los Angeles, California where it's warm all year! never any snow! just going to the beach and eating oranges and coconuts like some tropical island except it's right here in America, so nice the movie stars all go there to live (Rams leave Cleveland, Dodgers Brooklyn, Giants leave, go play games in light sunshine while rest of America glums in dusky snow), and kids there don't go to old rickety-tack amusement park of drooling old man arcade, clunking Ferris wheel and carousel that you wait for nine old cold months to open up, and even then you have to beg parents or sneak because every leather jacketed grease bully likes to hang out there and ogle girlflesh (I would have been there, like that, looking that vain look at cool moon of butt under folded shorts leg, not knowing why) (why anything?), Dr. Sax waiting over there, collar perked nose poked behind hot dog stand, slooth toothed, smell of vinegar rise from french fries, skies sloped and dark like his own hat brim—no, they got this place called Disneyland, sunshine in every crevice, eternal daylight funstuff world rides under water space jungle, everything like some previous movie adventure of Davey Crockett Jules Verne Swiss Family, amusement park of good clean racial kid memory, no slouch shouldered tobacco stained riderunner but shiny faced attendant with name tag says "Bobbi!"—Mom and Dad would even like to go! dream of every kid who ever sat in early dark evening eastern snowlight, be willing to sit in car for fifty hours quiet as bug and drive there! I saw it written on faces of my sister Nin's kids even in mild North Carolina—little does childmind know it's all facade of Total Police Authority hooking into Cable TV tube of brain.

Inside huge gate damn of people flow to Disneytram Disneyrail Disneybus under Mickey Mousehead flag flutter (in dead desert Santa Ana air, Raphael says little fan planted at top of every pole to flutter flags just so so you can see perfectly unfurled Disney insignia, Donald Duck Mickey Mouse and Goofy heads) Urso and Duluoz walk down replica turn of century Main Street America (last time anything was pure, before great wars, before birth of Duluoz)—too hot to continue even as all around us kids in cotton brained fever charge tugging Mom Dad past shops to rides!—we are lugging pot bellies and fat cells searching for Disney beer and can't find one anywhere! settling for Coke (can't buy water or cup, have to buy Coke) in which we pour from pints of bourbon bought in Colorado in fear of driving through Utah, but then facing same dryness of soul in California, Anaheim; now have enough energy to wander to Tinkerbell Castle which I see in all trueness was modeled after the Temple in old Salt Lake.

"The amazing thing is that this isn't even really here," says Urso, "but is beamed down via those crucifixes with naked girls that are orbiting the planet. They got these rays now, lasers, that can make you see and feel anything they want. This is where they test it out. They got one in Florida now too. Everything here's a fake of some other replica. They got Abe Lincoln here, Einstein, everybody."

"You sound like Plato," (who I had to read my freshman year at Columbia while meanwhile bashing my head working in cafeteria as well as football field, thinking at the time that I needed to contemplate him by late night reading lamp pipe puffing and now realizing best to read such stuff between head bashings after all).

"Plato didn't know shit about this. This is none of that silly metaphor shit. This *is* America. There's no God underneath this, no

Void. This is sitting on bombs and death gas. Mickey Mouse is death gas. Goofy's the A Bomb. Minnie Mouse is the fuckin CIA."

"Let's go on a ride."

"Another twenty years they're going to have a ride named after you, right here in Disneyland. Stick out your thumb while you're waiting in line, put you in a little convertible and drive through a diorama tour of America, Tony Bennet singing '*Je pense a Dean Moriarty*' out a speaker in back of your seat, Disney dancers bee-bopping in bobby socks to Rock'n'Roll on Main Street, sweepstakes to win a '56 Chevy, they'll give out abridged copies of *Road* without drugs or sex scenes as consolation prizes."

"Aah let's go on a ride."

"Okay, but first we have to get stoned, so we need a ride that only seats two."

Which is not easy, but we do find some kind of frog and toad ride, wags through London streets in dark with much jerking and sudden pop up lit up surprise chimney sweep and grave digger types, old maids with millions of cats, drunks, alley dogs, reminding me somewhat of old funhouse days walking ooshsquoosh on cushions dead bodies and trap door buzzers, though in those days you could knock around in funhouse all day and never come out, spend whole afternoons scaring pants off kindergarten kids in darkened halls; here you can't get out of the car and all the jerking makes it hard to hold joint and suddenly BANG through two doors ride is over and there we are at end of ride two fat old poets smoking pot with parent kid audience.

But I am well practiced from old days in San Francisco Renaissance when Total Police Authority first became aware of hipster under-current (not knowing we were holy and beatified and loved Americans who worked all day in Detroit sweat to build our Chevrolets ((and even Chevrolets themselves)) knowing only we did not like A-Bombs, tanks, full destructive employment, and so chose to remain unemployed), which meant I had to learn to eat joints.

Not that it matters because nobody notices anyway. Spend next couple hours wandering through Disneyland and waiting for rides which pretty much amount to theme roller coasters (only not so scary as old amusement park coasters because they have too much efficiency, zip up, zip down, no rickety-rackety plywood tower height on rotting wood scaffold, nothing to fear, being part of Urso's point which he reminds me everytime we whoosh and sloop up and down and over—"death via nullified negative capability" is how he puts it, and I'm thinking that the only change I notice in him in fifteen or so years ((besides fatter and toothless)) is that he uses bigger words between profanities).

So now we're dizzy and need a place to rest, but not some Disney bench in Fantasyland with screaming kids and french fries and Thought Police, but a place with grass and shade.

"I gotta headache. It's a death headache, a head death ache," says Raphael Urso, poet who brings back from dead Jack Duluoz to Disneyland to find death. Nothing to do but drag him to Pirates of Caribbean, at least a dark ride on cool water, lots of low yo-ho-ho's, rum drinking, innocuous pillaging pirate replicas, but too many of the statues remind Raphael of his relatives.

"I'm sick," says Urso. "This was a mistake."

"No mistake," I say. "I never got to do this while I was alive. This is the whitewash soul of fun under sweat of America who forgot her poemself. Think of the kids in Africa, China, Russia, Brazil, wishing they had this. Look at all these people of the U.S. and world here to get away and not think and forget for day their weary lives, and some great corporate chief building pirate robots and Goofy statues, hiring weary lived Americans and then selling amusement, taking profits and giving them to senators, presidents, yacht builders, bomb makers who hire more weary Americans who need to come here! bring children! and children's children! It's no different than toothpaste!"

"I gotta lay down," says Urso, holding head. "You're making me worse, that's what."

But where to lie down in Disneyland? I think maybe of going back to van, but then would roast in treeless parking lot tin can van oven (no place to hide) no shape to drive, no sense cracking head against ceiling of eternity, only thing to do is become, in this case, Disneyland ("Whoever is stiff and inflexible is a disciple of death.

Whoever is soft and yielding is a disciple of life," says the Tao) and remembering rucksack wineday afternoons and threat of alcohol blur cloud consciousness, only thing to do is find a place right here in Disneyland to keep drinking and best place is part of the scenery.

"Remember how many times yours truly saved you from beatings and police because of road knowledge of when to run and hide and where," I tell Raphael and take him arm over shoulder to Adventureland Jungle Ride.

"I don't want no more rides."

"But this one's slow enough to get out of," remembering from TV that unlike Pirate Ride where one boat follows another through cute swashbuckle scenes, Jungle Ride has hippos and gators slip out of water and appear for each boat, has to be triggered in turn everytime and so there must be time between each boat around bends to debark and make shore.

"We'll get all wet."

"What better?"

So we just make sure we're sitting in back of the boat. Take off from dock, round bend, see family of friendly natives waving, then not so friendly natives with spears, drums and voodoo hoots, great white hunter head pops out of cooking pot, Disney guide says for thousandth time that day that it's time to get moving on before we end up like him (plastic) (though by this time exactly my plan, hee-hee); guide spins wheel, (beautiful over-emphasized casual spin of wheel unconnected to rutter or boat, line of Disney boats on metal track into same adventureless adventure over and over, inevitably and innocuously into heart of Disney Darkness), elephant family appears heerunking on left, jipittering monkeys on right, boat turns around next bend and as hippo family appears out of water at right front of boat Urso and Duluoz slip off the back, hold breath till boat disappears then wade to shore, head out cross country through Disney jungle till we find friendly band of gorilla statues in stand of shade and sit down to dry off and drink ourselves sober, all being pretty private there behind that gorilla family except for every minute or so when new boat comes by and we have to listen to nearby speakers imitating chest pounding and hooting, and the resounding and requisite ooohs from passing boat, Disney guide saying those gorillas don't look too friendly and probably get less friendly the closer you get so better just move on around to next bend, every once in a while we do our own pounding and hooting too until Raphael thinks we can do it just as well as the speakers and rummages through weeds until they're found, whereupon he disconnects wires saying we'll just reconnect them when we get tired and of course we get tired of carrying the full responsibility of all that hooting and pounding pretty fast and soon enough we're hooting ourselves hoarse while Raphael can't figure out how to reconnect wires.

"Now what?" says I.

"Now we can't have a nap," says Raphael. "As soon as you're good at something somebody wants you to do it all fuckin day!"

No choice now but to walk right out there with the gorilla family and wave and pound and hoot for next boat (and somewhere in the history of this U.S. in the photo albums of lives—I think of the families of lives and the lives of families in the photo album histories of family vacations, family holidays, family America deeping itself in sad quiet Kodak page of moment, the father points at these photos to his kids ((bored kids who'd rather be watching giant space zapping robots on TV or teen-age Beverly Hills Barbie Dolls, but who in ten years twenty years will think their mother's breasts and father's love were just some dream and point at photos to their kids to bring it back)), the mother saying, this was *my* father, and this *his* mother, and we were at the park on the Fourth of July in 1942, and here, look what they wrote on this rock, their names, your names, Maggie Jo and Ti Bob, if we went back there we could find them—photographs! pictures! Polaroids of two old men hooting and pooting with the gorillas at Disneyland, one, unbeknownst, a ghost ((how long a way I've come to report him to myself)); there, in those stories of those dreams under the American blue dawn, the dawn of the land unceasing in the American soul and dream of foolish feeling, and that of course the only thing worthwhile, the heart and nothing else, my return is recorded too, dead and returned like Lucifer and Christ, amidst robot gorillas!) (maybe your Mom and Dad have that picture, go look and see).

By the time the next boat comes around bend we've given up hooting for haiku. We have arms around gorillas. Urso hugs gorilla baby. We are one big haiku shouting primate family. Drinking is okay. Bananas are okay. Tourists are okay. Disney guides okay. Everything holy and okay in Disneyland.

The poets drink with the gorillas
as the tourists
take their pictures!

Fantasyland moontrips.
One Valencia orange
in Anaheim!

Across the ocean
someone thinks of a bird
with guts and feathers!

Coming in emptyhanded,
going out emptyhanded.
What is your original face?

The moon is shining everywhere!

Methinks it the haiku that brings a boatload of Disney Police on next boat (or maybe that the last poem wasn't haiku at all but stolen saying from Seung Sahn) (just as well, we're almost out of booze), but when we head back overland we hear bullhorn and thrashing through weeds making it apparent we are being flanked! (and not just simple warning to remove ourselves, but asking us to give ourselves up for arrest!), two old Beats, one dying, one dead, being chased through the back country of Adventureland Jungle Ride! Disney dogs howling our subversive scent. But remembering what some Disney character himself would do, Swamp Fox, Davey Crocket, or old Zagg himself (me) lurking under Merrimack River Moody Bridge, Sax befriended and over shoulder sloophing (because he is a ghost who avoids and he who avoids is holy) I guide panting Raphael on precise backtrack to place of original debarking.

"Let's just give up," screams Raphael. "What're they going to do, lock us in Frontierland fucking jail? I don't want to get wet again!"

"Never place yourself in the hands of authority. You of all people should know."

"I want to die!"

"You'll feel better after we've escaped."

"I don't care! I want to die now!"

"Only somebody who's never been dead would say that."

"Aah, you don't know nothin about it."

Nonetheless it only takes one shove to get him in the water and back out to other side where we follow the river straight to the entrance where Raphael tells waiting families to keep their children away from the sides of the boats because it's easy to fall out, and as they can see, old people should be careful too.

"Let's get out of here," he says.

"Nah, they'll just be waiting for us at the gate. We have to hide out in the park and let the heat of the incident cool in their minds till we're reduced to anecdote."

"We'll be buried in Disneyland!"

"Yes, they'll put all Beat writers here, like Tombstone Boothill graveyard in Frontierland. Garden. Hubbard. Urso. Duluoz."

"Ryder. O'Hara."

"I don't want to be buried with O'Hara."

"Like you got a choice. They won't be real graves anyway."

And in Fantasyland, reborn in the body of myself unchanged, only older as I'd be if I'd not died at all, I sit with Raphael Urso (should I be with someone else, Johnnie? Irwin? Cody? — I should be with Cody, but how do the dead find the dead? —) pondering thought of fake grave, feigned death—why have I returned? why die? why born at all?—knowing in the first place that the only thing to do is make your living and eat your meals and wait for the darkness (the darkness I've been denied) (because God isn't Pooh Bear after all but editor of *Time* Magazine, made me write this book of built-in irony to boost me Proustian—who cares? says I still, irony just some adjective for things over-pressed, tee-hee, it being easier to laugh at critics and self as well on this side of death), knowing I am just on some Bardo journey to grave from wrong direction of life (and wrong end of country!) what else to do but rest and wait?

We sit on white bench at white table with white umbrella, teen-ager in red, white, and blue cap (name tag says Ted!), still has acne, selling Disney Burgers and Fantasy Fries to Mom and Dad, two kids, one boy, one girl, Mickey Mouse and Daisy Duck balloons, young Chicano kid shovels trash into scooper dust pan with broom (brown-eyed, Indian blooded, sad heartbrown face of all Mexico, he's out here cleaning trash in hot sun while acne Anglo teen-ager works burgers in shade), across the way Magic Mountain Space Ride rumbles while children of the USA scream their screaming American delight of parents who can afford $20 a head to get in Disneyland (but when babe cries at night for Mommie from nightmare and grows from sad innocence of joy to tragic sadness of life which is just some other way of saying death, the underground rotting of flesh, the saddest dream of crying night from which no one wakes, the dollar sign soothes not, who's to deny this white child any joyflash moment in that face?) this is the sadness on every side of everything; I go over to Mickey Mouse hat booth and get two Mickey Mouse hats, get names embroidered on back, one says Jack, one Raphael, knowing that no one has ever been arrested in America wearing Mickey Mouse ears, and we put them on, the two fattest mice in Magic Kingdom.

13

But I underestimate the tenacity of Disney Police who have called in Outside Authority, local Anaheim County Sheriff thugs and high booted helmet goggled California State motorcycle leadheads, nothing better to do on June day (spent morning cracking jaywalkers on Manchester Blvd. then got in cars heading out for free coffee and donuts, probably would've ignored Disney distress call anyway if it'd caught them before that coffee made 'em jagged nerved and needy to squelch some flagrant innocuity) nothing better to do than lift night sticks at fat mouse-eared writers, surround us with guns, suggest we come along peacefully because we've done enough damage, scared too many children—no use telling them they're the only ones with weapons and there wasn't any commotion at all here in Fantasyland until they showed up, though I do anyway, which means I get my nuts grabbed extra hard while we're frisked and cuffed, then paraded out of Disneyland in long line of Disney golf carts, Mickey Mouse head insignia on side of each one like Red Star, White Star, Swastika, Rising Sun (you choose)—Raphael says "Don't talk to 'em, they're stupid jars of dirt," which is probably why we get Mickey Mouse hats knocked off with night sticks once they get us in police cars and out of park.

14

We're booked at the Anaheim County Jail (another place to look for face of the returned Duluoz, fingerprints too), though I do not give real name or I.D.; get railroaded for vagrancy, drunken disorder, several counts of assault (on police, children, gorillas) verbal and otherwise, lewd and licentious behavior, violation of open bottle law, enough to put us away for years except jail is already full. We get off with room and board for one night on the tax payers of California, making me realize once again how little we need taxes, police, jails—all real criminals do not get caught, even searched for, anyway (insurance and oil executives who own your own backyard, buy off auto manufacturers, hire sledgehammers to go out and beat the feet of Americans scared by American Press TV radio billboards, ((owned by Exxon or Wheatland or Prudential or Hearst)) into believing that without either one they'd perish into nothingness, be unable to drive to Disneyland, get sued by each other into bankruptcy, have to live on rice and beans and not be able to send kids for pedigree of illiteracy at State U, get out and join great American unhappy desire life, drink in polluted air, water, stop smoking cigarettes, fly in airplanes, go to movies, live forever until the scythe comes anyway) it's a story of the world where only the poor go to jail, and who to tell it when same corporations own publishing, TV, Hollywood? poor American workhead (you) escapes from work-a-day job life to be entertained by same people scaring him into life of purchase for his own good, worst of it all being that it's all so well intentioned (and this from same Duluoz who once in youth of post-war Forties dreamed of going to Hollywood and making millions as script writer, writing movies about Joyce, Dostoyevsky, Proust) (part of reason I stopped being read in America, told truth and ceased to be entertaining, so who will publish this?) phooey, from the grave it don't matter and the grave is all there is—lucky for Thoreau he didn't have to come back and see (aah Duluoz, more irony ironing, tell it to Mémêre who ironed all her life, iron me that!).

Urso uses one phone call to call Bull Hubbard who is real reason we started trip to LA in first place, Hubbard and Urso having to give some poetry reading somewhere in Venice Beach the next night, then go up coast, read in Fresno, San Francisco, living Beat artifacts—"aah," I tell 'em right there when Hubbard shows up, "you guys would be nothin if I wasn't dead."

"And even better off if you were never around in the first place," says Raphael.

"You don't use logic based humor on a drunken fool," Hubbard tells Urso from front seat of limo where he rides with driver. He still speaks with that long drawn out drawl like drawing his voice through a base fiddle and a duck before it comes out all nasty and thoughtful with the weight of every idea in the history of Western thinking. From back seat he looks like a light bulb, bald, ears, hat, his very head, as you might say, a cartoon metaphor for having ideas.

"Irwin stole everything from me," I'm forced to tell them. "O'Hara. McLear too, what little he has."

"Me too," says Raphael. "Never fuckin had an original thought."

"I wasn't going to say it in front of you."

"Eat the corn outta my shit. That's Beckett, if you didn't know."

"It's Tennessee Williams in *Night of the Iguana*," drones Bull, "and your version is a bad paraphrase."

"Who gives a shit," says Raphael.

"I learned things from dead writers."

"Those are the best kind," says Hubbard.

"A couple things from Japhy and Bull."

"What did you learn from your Mother, that's what I want to know," says Raphael.

"How to love Jesus, if that ain't enough."

15

"Nobody gives a shit what anybody knows," says Hubbard after long time in quiet air cooled dark limo ride through sunlight dry California valley, riding through sea of dozen laned freeway, car jammed, smog fooped, fop and mup of LA foofing, hair, beard, phone talking in speeding wheeled car cubicle, spread of suburban lived sprawl between cement (little did I know I'd drawn perfect replica of LA freeways in abstract doodle drawn back in Cody days *Visions of Neal* ((furbishoos and finishes, or is this diddling?)), not published of course till 1972 after my death; you can find it on page 337 of the first hardback edition).

Sometime later out of dark of car Hubbard's voice floats again (frontward, out of light bulb, drawning off windshield and caroming into back seat like unmailed letter voice), to no one, (Raphael now asleep, and myself, though I spoke to Bull several times in my life, and again at present, and though I heard him speak plenty of times, would be hard pressed to say he ever spoke to me).

"Nobody reads, nobody thinks, and who cares, the world ended a long time ago but you had to read about it to find out."

Then quiet again till we are in Venice, little hotel at foot of Washington Street and Venice Pier where we follow Hubbard out of car like Three Old Stooges Eenee Meenee minus Moe, and into hotel suite, shades down, Hubbard even has rocking chair, picks up phone for room service and orders pitcher of extra dry martinis.

"The trouble with all this pre-apocalyptic garbage, right into the eighties, is that it misses the whole boat. The world was already dead spiritually and culturally after World War Two. A nuclear war would just kill people," says Bull apocalyptically.

"Animals," says Urso.

"We don't need the bomb for them, we'll get 'em all anyways, except for rats and roaches, pigeons, sea slugs."

"You obviously missed my adamantine pun on the Buckley Show," I tell Hubbard. "Adamantly post-atom Adam post-Eden Adam up and at 'em Edie Adams."

"The only way to gain any intellectual respect is to be unreadable," says Bull, "then nobody has to read you, which is what they do anyways, not read."

"Nah, you just do this new minimal shminimal stuff, you know, third person dramatic, open ended, no qualified dialogue, lots of blank space like Hemingway, if you want to be artsy you go present tense or second person—easy reading, easy to recognize cuz you sound like everybody else—the critics will think you're profound because you kept your trap shut and let 'em think what they wanted, and grateful you didn't make 'em read many pages, words, ideas."

"What anybody thinks they understand is simply dangerous," says Bull.

"Look at this Dick Chevrolet. First he writes a perfect sentence, then he writes another perfect sentence. Wot a crock. 'The cat is on the mat.' There's a perfect sentence, and you ain't got to be Lood-vig Wittgenstein to understand that. What the hell ain't a perfect sentence? All sentences are perfect or they ain't sentences and who cares. God gives it to you and it comes out."

"It's parody, even if unintended, self or otherwise," croaks Bull."

"Or these rich kids writing about drugs."

"Coke," says Urso. "They just wanna be a part of something. An underground. But the rich ain't an underground. And besides, nothin gets into print unless it's been dead for years. Look at *Road*."

"The only good idea is a dead idea," says Bull.

"The thing about the American underground now," says Raphael, "is everybody's in it, because everybody's hiding. You put on your coat and tie and go to work selling boat engines or wiener casings or some fucking tiny part of a weapons system, but you *think* whatever you want, especially on weekends. You're against drugs in the ghetto, but it's okay for you, even if you vote Republican and get your drugs from the Communists in Columbia subsidized by the Fascists in Venezuela who get their money from the CIA fighting Communists in Nicaragua, or you just do prescription drugs or cheat on your taxes, don't fuckin tell me. Everybody's part of the whole thing but because they're an individual they ain't the whole thing so they're against the whole thing, that evil big thing that they aren't because they're an individual and they're good and they're against it. That's the New American Underground."

"The Great New American Underground!" says I.

"That's the audience," says Raphael.

"The only good audience is a dead audience," says Hubbard.

"Phooey, I just read that crazy South American stuff now."

"Whose?"

"Mostly my own. I got a lot of time on my hands," (and now, minimal subliminal ishkabibinal criminal, I should interject short observation of Hubbard eye twitch, Urso belly hair, glint of prescient dew on martini pitcher, some objective cor-Elliotive where outer becomes inner and scene turns into metaphor—ah, Duluoz, you could 'a played football for Columbia).

"Man, I thought you were asleep during the Buckley Show," says Raphael.

"Not the part where I talked."

But about now Bull is falling asleep in mid-drawl (he's already said all this stuff a million times in all his books anyways, starting about thirty years ago).

"Okay," I say, "before all this ends there's something I always wanted to do and that's shoot an apple off Bull's head."

"Fine," says Bull from his sleep.

"All you need is a gun and an apple," says Raphael.

"Order 'em from room service," says Bull.

That seems improbable enough, but this is Los Angeles Venice Beach in America and it's only a gun, not something dangerous like baloney or a cigarette. I call up room service and say, "Please bring an apple and a gun up to Mr. Hubbard's room please."

"What kind?"

"Red Delicious."

"Of gun."

"Make it a .38," says Bull in prescient drawl of slumber.

"A .38," says I.

"Okay, that'll be about a half-hour."

Which isn't long to wait, considering. In half-hour bellboy appears at door with apple and .38 on tray.

"You have to sign for the apple," bellhop says, "but the gun's just a loaner to

Mr. Hubbard from the manager."

"That's fine," I say signing check for the apple (expensive at $3), "he can have the gun back in an hour."

I put the apple on Bull's head.

"Think about this," says Raphael. "You shoot that gun you'll wake him up."

"I been back from the dead in America for three days and I haven't got to do one thing I wanted to do when I was here the first time except for drink and that's something I wanted to *stop* doing."

"He paid our bail and gave us a limo ride."

"It'll only hurt if I wound him."

"He doesn't get his sleep he'll miss the reading. That puts too much pressure on me. I ain't the straight man."

"No one's ever been killed by a dead man, there's Existential precedent." I step back as far as I can to the corner of the room to make it worth shooting. Bull keeps hooting softly out nose and giving slight lip blubber of jaw drop rocking chair sleep and I have to time shot between oozes of air. It's a big apple, almost as big as Bull's head.

It's one of those great moments near death like my time on the *Dorchester*, innocent blond German torpedo youth, submarined, waiting to blow out brains of innocent Americans just doing their bit, transferring war materials to England where mothers and babes wait under impersonal bombs, a big fight where everybody gets bloody nose of death, red dawn death, blue day death, sunset death stretching on horizon reaching purple to starry death black night, all to bring us where we are today, Nicaragua death, El Salvador death, death Cambodia, death Iraq, death Iran, death waiting in silos of wealth under ever waving grain, what then a little playful death dealing between old friends? Raphael, poet of *Birthday Party of Death* understands this completely, he sits down on bed.

"Aah, you're not Duluoz, you're just some nut."

It's a slippery gun in slippery hands of sweat (haven't even touched one in thirty-five years when held Mill Valley security guard job with Demi Bleu, and even then just wore it on hip, never touched the thing), but remember Navy training days of exhale and squeeze, don't pull; don't even know why I want to do this except it seems so appropriate, leave Bull with gun powdered apple core smell of ghost. I think I have pretty good aim but just as trigger squeezes down Bull startles in chair and head pops up where apple should be—to late to stop trigger—apple falls from Bulls head to shoulder, trigger trips, hammer goes down and then there's a loud CLICK!

Nothing. No Bullets in gun.

"Think I'm a goddamn fool," says Hubbard barely opening eyes. "Who the hell are you anyway."

"Aah," says I, "you don't want to know."

"You're right," says Bull, sometime later, after little more doze in dark, though soon enough we're all dozing old and dozed asleep in Venice Beach, lights out konked out how and where we're all alike and close to God, Timeless, it's Tangier, Orizaba Street Mexico City, New Orleans, San Francisco—I'm reminded that we are all ghosts, some living, some waiting, some gone—we aged angels sleeping in heart of desolation, together, solitude.

16

It isn't the old ghost of young Duluoz but new ghost of old Duluoz returned who no longer sleeps in corner stupor of wine remembering babe remembering all—yellow sunlight through shade in brown room, and brown the color of memory—Bull Hubbard on rocking chair dreaming omniscient sleep, Raphael Urso sprawled on bed of sweat in innocent sweet betrayal of consciousness, the best of all young contradictions grown old wise mean joyous absurd and deep in life's illusion—some of us are doomed to write it down, the metaphor for the metaphor of the Void, full voidless and empty as God's face (happiness) —if you read closely then life is just a story too, pace and timing, foreshadowing love pain, every concrete thing an image (for this we thank Dr. Williams)—think about it, when is it time for the ghost of Duluoz to leave this scene? Now.

William Burroughs

Who wants to unpack a suitcase of shit. When there's not even anything in there you want.

The only lump of truth in this whole shitsack is that whoever wrote this *didn't* read any of Joy Johnson's memoir. She's the only editor I know who's published anything about Kerouac, and Corso would know that anyway. She slept with Kerouac off and on for a year. She probably really loved the bastard, poor woman.

But she didn't know whether to hate Kerouac or bake him cookies, neither of which are inherently boring in and of themselves without bad writing, or interesting in and of themselves without good writing. It isn't life, it's literature, and ambivalence is simply a means to an end.

Any sophomore can imitate Kerouac, or Hemingway, or anybody else for that matter, Joyce, anybody. Who did it first. That's all that counts, and everything else is after the fact. If I remembered every bum that Corso dragged in off the street I wouldn't have time for memories of my own.

Kerouac is dead for Christ's sake. Deader than a year before he was born. He wrote plenty of material. Anybody can read it. Go read it. But Jack Kerouac is dead. Leave him alone.

Gregory Corso

Disneyland is Death, I'll give him that. Dead things alive, living things dead. It's the world upside down. But I've never been there. I'm like the Pope. I just know this stuff.

Even if I have, so what? Poets have to wash their clothes. They have to shit. They have to do things like everybody else. The difference is, because they touch it, it's sublime. That's the difference. It's a matter of essence, like fucking light. I'm not shitting you. You can't change it.

Okay, so let's say this. Kerouac came back from the dead. When was it? 1982. I met him at Naropa. We drove to Disneyland, got drunk with the gorillas, ended up in jail, Burroughs got us out and Kerouac tried to shoot an apple off his head, the whole deal is true, Vegas, the pictures, everything. Everything you read here was true. He came back. I'm a witness. What does that change? That's right. Not a fucking thing.

17

Two things different about Venice Beach Los Angeles California 1982: more rich, more poor, though also new street drug called *crack* or *rock* or just plain *C*, some smoking version of cocaine; coke not being much the drug of choice in our day because we were more utilitarian about getting hyped up or inebriated, using drugs for personal insight or prolongation of long bouts of dialectic or days at typewriter or occasional mystic elevation on toilet seat with pad and pen or Bible (this of course the scatology and eschatology of Dr. Sax, boozeling the roofless night of conscience constellated stars, the flushing of mind), or booze plain and simple when the thought of thought too much to think (if you meet the Buddha on a road, kill him, if you find your mind conscious, put it to sleep) (if our minds are what makes us God-like, why sleep a third of our lives? why be dead for most of eternity? God loves us sleeping innocent like babes, don't be fooled); when we wanted to get *up* we stayed up for a long time cheap, took speed—coke more of a musician drug, jazz blues needs those downs as bad as highs to keep low souled and moodfull for inspiration—anyway as you walk up from beach now all the ramshackle shacks of old honky-tonk Venice now cute little white beach houses like *Architectural Digest*, *pleine air* California light, banana trees growing in skylight foyer, baby blue Porsche or burgundy Jaguar shining in carport like Easter egg.

Go up few blocks from beach to old West Washington Blvd. and cross over Electric Avenue and find yourself plap in middle of black and Mexican ghetto, dealers in streets on bikes yelling "hoop-hoop-halloo I got *C* here for you," people drive up in very same Easter eggs, Porsche Mercedes Jaguar from down near beach, from Beverly Hills, buy cocaine (take it home and get held up by brother-in-law of dealer). In alleys, sad old Negroes, eyes drooped, pants dropped, piss and shit next to crack smokers staggering from fences in foogled frenzy, eyes folded into head, while to north enlightened wealth of Santa Monica glistens on Palisades, throwing smell of money shadow, and boozshwa new Marina insinuating its whiteness to south, the hovering temptation of America want it got it spend it conduits of money, sea of LA sparkle around sad island of Mexican families packed eight to a room, fathers go out in cars to get drunk (only way to get away from wife\kids) drop Bud cans from cars blasting Salsa till dawn, till wives come out, pick up cans, slap husbands over shoulders and drag them in and clean them up, bring them out an hour later (child troop straggling behind), scrubbed shaved lunch bucketed, send them out to work again (better life than in old Mexico, living in cardboard shack in dry river bed, carless), black mothers in blue dawn leaving kids with grandma to go out and work in front of some computer terminal disease, minimum wage life bleed to AT&T, while old Negro men play dominoes in park, dozens of Mexicans kick soccer ball lunch break, bands of Negro teen-agers in white shirts and black pants jump out of trucks, vans, blasting Hip-Hop, carry black spray paint (walls everywhere covered with strange hieroglyph swastikas under initials, VSLC for Venice Sho Line Crips, some gang like Dago gangster gangs of old, control drug and prostitution territory, sweep by in cars with small machine guns like the CIA), carry small pipes for crack smoke, come in and out of rundown houses, CRACKIN, black whores hanging like black skeletons from rails, while on opposite corner drug addicts of another generation (mine) drag their slow ass horse legs through street in front of junk yard where they sleep in abandoned bus, windows painted black or cardboard covered, and a young Mexican woman, four knee-high kids around her tugging on skirt, sweeps dirt of dirt front yard, old dog with watermelon tumor sleeps on steps. It's as sad as Harlem has ever been sad.

Of course I'm a bum and safe, on foot, old (nobody comes to this neighborhood to rob nobody anyways, everybody's already poor, and if you held up any of those Easter eggs it'd be bad for local business, besides, five thousand replicas of me in streets anyway, lying in front of post office, bank, bakery, hardware store, lined up in wheelchairs, crutches, barefoot, begging for change), and I'm deciding how to get to train station bus station to head to San Francisco when I see white man standing in front yard of house in middle of block waving a bowling ball. Only thing to do is go up and talk to him.

"You going bowling?"

"No, I don't bowl. This is just a show of force."

"Who you showing?"

"Anybody who's watching."

"You're not afraid of them machine guns?"

"You ever been hit by a bowling ball?"

"You live here?"

"Can I afford to live anywhere else?"

"Because you're some kind of artist?"

"Maybe I'm a writer?"

"That's a good answer."

"Thank you, this question asking was getting me tired."

"I did some writing."

"I bet. I bet you got a screenplay right there in your bag."

"No, I dreamed of writing screenplays for a short while, even wrote one, but nothing happened."

"It's hard to get things done in your dreams. I started one myself but I realized I couldn't write stupid enough."

"Well what did you write?" says I.

"Wrote the true story of my life set in my home town."

"Where's that?"

"Youngstown."

"Can't say I've ever been through there."

"You can't go through," he says, "all the roads only go around it."

"I never knew that."

"You've never been there, how could you know? How could anybody? Unless they read the books? But if I'm lucky I'll never finish it and it will never be published. The story goes on for pages and pages, it goes on forever until I die."

"Sometimes it goes on after you die."

"That's good news because several of my characters have died but they're still in the story."

With that he popped that bowling ball onto the tip of his index finger and gave it a spin, let it roll down his right arm and over his shoulders to the end of his left arm where he kept it spinning on the other index finger. There were probably any number of people right down on Venice Beach at that minute, roller skating and acrobating and some of them even juggling, some of them even juggling bowling balls, real professional performers, who couldn't come close to what this guy could do simply for self defense in his front yard, a bowling ball Buddha mad saint.

He continued, "I learned this from my father who bowled and walked around the house all day pumping a bowling ball until it became like part of his arm. Kept it up long after he stopped bowling."

"You used to bowl?"

"No, never did. I was a bowling machine mechanic once, but that's as close as I got."

Just then a beautiful woman appears at screen door of house, dark eyes like world misery but blue with joy at center, slender legs and a softness that turns street silent and brown, on her hip is beautiful chubby girl babe of blonde hair blue eyes but same darkness of lash and brow—the sun comes out and turns us all yellow—and I am reminded that all saints are proven by beautiful and holy women who hold them in the night and spawn warm Tao Tao-less freedom, look at Japhy, and this maybe reason I am back, because of all the holy women I left Yanging, maybe I am trodding back through America until I meet them all, all at once, and at that moment I'll learn everything and be free to come back as female myself, holy to some Buddha like this one who writes life forever.

"Is this a crack dealer?" says woman.

"No, it's just a homeless bum who like all homeless bums is welcome here anytime for a short while."

"I wrote some books too," I say. "Some even got published."

"That's too bad," says the woman.

"What were they?" says man.

"*Road* was the most famous but not the best."

"You must be Duluoz," says he.

"That's right," says I.

"I read you back in the days when I was shooting heroin and reading Kierkegaard. I see you've stopped publishing the last few years"

"He's dead," says Madonna saint holding babe.

"I love Mamma! I love Dadda!" says round child of innocent (cynical) bowling ball Venice saints.

"We're all dead from day one," I tell them what they already know, "it just takes different forms."

So these are the angels who drive the dead Duluoz back into downtown Los Angeles to catch the San Francisco bus.

18

You never know when you're going to have to get off a bus even if you have enough salami sandwiches to make it to the moon—and I had plenty, my angels sent me off with stick of salami and loaf of sourdough, bottle of $1.99 French Bordeaux, all from some strange California grocery (in Culver City across from movie lot) only sells food wholesome certified natural and cheap—naturally cured salami from naturally cured cows, waited for them to die natural death before using meat, probably drying on cow bones while still alive—traditional Duluoz bus lunch except Duluoz himself would have bought sliced white bread and sliced salami, which I told them, and they told me, yes, but it's 1982. How does that change salami sandwiches? I say, and am told to eat it with my eyes closed (like the blind men and the elephant), and not wanting to end up like main character in old morality play, mysterious gift giving angels riddling me to eternity by car ride, I remain silent, (angels being porpoises of ethereal sea, have own purposes, and when take you drowning to land you don't follow them back into the ocean ((you don't squeak their language, hee-hee)), take your salami and run)—swimsical.

I get off bus in old San Luis, wander to train yard and remember old days of Dharma wandering freight hopping of Southern Pacific Zipper Midnight Ghost, bum of Saint Teresa, Japhy, Cody Fresno days dropping like heart beat under train wheels, ka-thunk ka-dick ka-thunk ka-dick, Ooowing through Time night, empty boxcars loaded with ghosts of bumsaints only, flatcar ride daylight, gondola full rainsack coal bottom, brakeman eyeglint (of brakeman once I glinted myself in old San Jose), switch throw and rumble earth like old Pluto or Dis under rainbow earth, earth bottom, earth ground, bottoms up earth bowels carried to burn light of America home pies pork chops, heat, (TV!), astrodomes, all of America rolling by, the goods of American heart too heavy to fly, too big for trucks, only the trains which now lie on side of yet another road, head turned in droop of death like Irwin's sunflower, giant iron ghosts on raindark rail (kud-think kid-thunk, everything ends, kud-think kid-thunk, everything ends, even if skies and planes kud-think kud-fly kid-thunk, kud-fall kud-think), you trains, as Irwin says, be trains!

In distance on track stands trainman, lanterned, white T-shirt bright shine over rail as sunset streams him across metal track of train yard stretching all the way to me, arm hang, legs stretched in reverse V, swinging light at nothing in sudden yard quiet dusk funnel, silence, whole earth now shaking in silence—it's Cody! ghost of train, rail walking Cody of light beaming me to him (and why not, why should I who set out for Denver and for Lowell ending up in Disneyland via Urso and San Luis Obispo via angels doubt what I see?) Cody.

Down abandoned track I see him behind light in black night rush and sudden crazy fog drizzle while off in distance over dark coast peaks heat lightning streaks sky; legs of piston dash, roads of muscle arm, amputated thumb tip held up! Cody! I adjust hat, lift bag and walk to him. "Jack old boy," he'll say, "let's me and you go shoot pool, get jobs as bellboys at the Biltmore, run old elevators all day, get drunk with butchers and stooges of Fresno night. Yeah, let's go! What's to stop us now? What's a few days of death in the re-run of eternity? Why over-affirm the negative? Who cares what we are, we know what we're not or we don't. We're accidents falling into a moment of motivated clarity. Let's go!" He in front of light now propped on railroad tie behind him, I see him illumined, smile jagged. Cody! Then light goes out. Old Mexican Indian stands there scratching beard.

"Thought you were somebody else," says he.

"Well I thought *you* were somebody else."

"I probably am."

This Indian has hands like sledge hammer heads on the end of old arms that used to be able to lift them, but now old with tendon and bone, burned leather skin, thin white hair short hair head, sunken jawed, thumbs parting from fingers like crab claws, he says, "You got anything to eat?"

I bring out my salami and bread and Bordeaux and we sit under abandoned water tower, watch listen to rain night old metal groan, indigence indigenous, indigents indignance, Indian indigo indignity indignant night (one old French Canuck too), I notice hanging from belt of mysterious salami sharer (who for a moment was Cody Pomeray), flag of Mexico and Our Lady of Guadalupe key chain with single key, the same as old Indian who slept next to me on bus to Juarez.

"Were you on the bus up to Juarez?" I ask.

"It's possible," he says. He rolls a cigarette and though I haven't smoked in years (except one on truck ride with Buddha who said everything was lousy) I share it with him, get orgasmic blast of pure smoke headspin from plain old tobacco high. It all tastes so delicious with the smoky salami and burnt wine and sour bread, trickle of strange summer desert rain, cool soft wind of wet breath earth, the hollow howling of empty trains and bang clatter of train yard, the best meal I've ever had, I think, live or dead.

"And when I saw you here from the distance I thought you were an old friend."

"Maybe I was," says he. "Maybe I'm everyone you've met. If life is a dream, what is death but a dream of death, and if there's no one to dream the dream, then who is fooling who?"

"You're just a mysterious old Indian bum. You're in some mysterious old Indian bum club and you all carry that key chain."

"That's right," he says. "You got it."

"You going to catch a freight?"

"Maybe."

"I rode some freights myself. I used to catch the Zipper here."

"The Ghost."

"That's right. But you have to catch it at midnight."

"No matter where you catch it," says he.

"Okay," I say, taking more of that cigarette, "that's not true but I'll buy it."

"That's why it's the Midnight Ghost."

"Aah, it probably doesn't even exist anymore."

"That's probably true. Like your friend."

"Like me," I tell him. "I'm here but I don't exist. I came back from the dead to be a metaphor for everybody and they don't even know it."

"It's probably for the best then."

"Maybe."

"Maybe you have to write it down."

"Maybe I do."

"Maybe I'm the Midnight Ghost," says Indian bum.

"Maybe you are."

"You have to ride me all the way to the sunrise."

"How could I do that? The Ghost only goes north."

"For you, anything. You going up to San Francisco?"

"Why not?"

"Because when you go back to where everyone knew you, everyone remembers and no one recognizes. It's a trick the past plays on the real."

"That so?"

"You don't have to be a ghost to know it."

"What do you have to be?"

"Observant."

"Nonetheless," I tell him, "I'm heading up to old Frisco to mull in streets that still smell like won-ton and slaughtered duck. I'm going to drink Irish coffee and watch old bar philosophers play chess."

"You're going so you can find your own smell on things you left behind."

That old Indian had a metal cup that he left out in the rain and now he had it filled with rain water and brought it back under the tower; we shared some of that rain water which was delicious and cold as the space between stars.

"Then I'm going to Denver to shoot pool with old men who were boys when Cody stalked the halls, gonna stop in Lawrence, Kansas and shoot an apple off Bull Hubbard's head this time, and then I think I'm gonna just take off straight for Mexico and bury my head, never come back here. Where you going?"

"I'm going to go up into the hills and point."

"I did that once."

"You can't do it enough."

"But you can't point at anybody or anything or for anybody."

"You don't have to tell me. But sometimes, somebody sees you."

"And they lock you up, or worse they make up stories about you and make you famous."

"You can't do anything about that," says the old Indian.

"No, you can't," says I.

He gets up and puts his cup in his pocket. "Where did you get that food?"

"Do your kind of Indians believe in angels?" I ask him.

"If we have to."

"Well that's where I got it from."

"It tasted like it," he says. He walks out from under the water tower and into that drizzle. "It's a nice rain to walk in, like rain from a blue moon," and he disappears into the dark.

19

I don't wait for a freight, I take rain walk back to bus station where that Frisco bus is still sitting in its canopied row of silverblue buses, lights of little terminal shining up from black asphalt in glisten of water and oil, monoxide fog fumes from bus pipes like cold winter night in any bus terminal in any American town, that bus will soon be warm and moving inside its fogged windows, just groan and motion and who knows what's going on or where we're really going, you just end up somewhere, and that's why night time is the best time to bus travel, especially in the rain and fog.

Myself I end up in Oakland dawn dawdle, buy pack of cigarettes and stand outside station, then walk down street into tenement houses, window blown, door painted, gang hieroglyphic, bums in stuporous stoops stooping out dawnlight from eyes, heads tucked, mostly all black, nothing anywhere but this poor tenement desolation and only worth mentioning because followed by gleaming ride over Bay Bridge with morning sun shining off white San Francisco so much as to make you wince, all that whiteness stretched on hills, urbantine downtown skyward stretch, white pyramided (hieroglyphless), looks like city from Krypton that got shrunk by evil green Braniac (strange electrodes on bald head) and kept in bottle by Superman in Arctic Fortress, make building repairs with tweezers, it's that delicate and neat, hard to find bums anywhere anymore, even in Mission, not even sleeping on buses or subway, subway so silver looks like you'd put it on your dinner table—oh Ma! how can I eat with this subway!—in fact no attendants in it at all, everything transacted by robot machines, get directions, change, ticket, entrance, robot info voice floats among us sad biological bodies lugging our personalities, cells, problems, loves, nobody poor enough in sight to give a dollar for cheap wine. Where'd they all go? To Oakland!

I walk up red bricked Market Street, shiny tiny stored, delis, smoke shops, coffee bars, clean windows with clean white black silver technological things inside, walk in there with a gnat on you and TV camera spots it, insecticide pours out of shower embedded in ceiling and you're back on the street guileless and parfumed, dangerous to all life including yourself, then up Grant Ave. to never changing Chinatown and on Sacramento St. just follow the crowds of Chinese down to little basement family Chinese restaurant, only white man in the place so I know it must be good, and fill up on Mongolian beef, fried rice and Kung Pao chicken, plenty of green tea, what a breakfast like days of old!—makes me want to find little Chinese girl and settle down, breed up brood of little Duluoz Francoamericanuck-gooks—but there is always something to remind you of the futile sadness of life like little girl at table across room with great burn scars across face, sits with family tries to smile, be normal, but what life awaits? here I am back in San Francisco in sympathy, which any Buddhist or Beat knows to be the middleless center of all virtue (only thing I ever professed and thing most lost, even in my day, Beat getting confused with lifestyle of parties and wealthy disdain of America that I, Duluoz, sympathized and loved, certain parties courting yours truly in thinking I documented their lives, another Lost Generation only with different name, something college educated journalists forced to read Gatsby twelve times at Yale Columbia Berkeley could understand, amoral love lust sensual vacuity that I never sought; like Cody I just wanted to find a girl, have house, car, family, write novels about sweet smalltown love, death, sorrow, turkey dinners) how do we all start out as children, sweet mothered babes, and end up like we do?

And now North Beach full of black and white tile floored piano bars, have to pay just to get in.

And Urso and Hubbard will be giving a reading that afternoon at the Keystone jazz club and you have to pay to get in to that too! $11!

Can't get into the Savoy Tivoli, it's packed with boys in polo shirts, girls in Zorro blouses, everybody drinking French water (and even I know about all the nuclear power plants over there leaking their subatomia into water table, making me admit for moment that maybe Urso is right, it's all pre-apocalyptic, everybody wants to walk around with nuclear explosion inside, don't want to be left out).

In Vesuvio's I take balcony table that looks out over Chinatown alley to Bright Lights Book Store, over Columbus to Broadway and girlie show vendors working tourists on sidewalk. Old Chinaman with cane gets off bus and heads down alley to steamed pork bun bakery on Grant St. right around corner, I can tell, he has pork bun walk, head tilted forward like baby, nose out to waft, cane flapping at side behind momentum. Little beat chick beats feet outside bookstore handing out copies of own poetry, got some kind of tights on underneath raggedy frilled petticoat skirt, black T-shirt, black Chinese slipper shoes, long red hair up in ponytail on very top of head (I know it's poetry because I've got a copy of it right here in my hand, called *Outlaw Marriage*, mostly about connubial and pornographic interludes with space creatures—gave her $1, opened book and read a few poems, she called them prose poems but they looked like chapters to me, and told her she should send it to Bull Hubbard, looked like it was right up his alley, she said a friend of hers already did and Bull called on the phone, told her she'd written the greatest book in the history of the planet, then she called him a perverted faggot and hung up —) she's pure and obscure on corner of Columbus and Broadway (like anyone, I says to her, ever reads Hubbard).

Then across alley on second floor of Bright Lights I see the head of Larry O'Hara, unmistakable manicured beard tracing down from balding head, head thrust forward but never enough to get out from under thrusting brow, some young couple up there with him, look like tour guides to the Mormon Temple, man with dark suit white shirt tie, woman in neat skirt and shoes everything just so like she's about to sell Larry encyclopedias. Lights go down but I can still see through window that they're looking at slides from slide projector, pictures of paintings, can't quite make them out, lots of swirly reds and blues. Then they're done and next thing they're downstairs and out (don't buy book from poet on street) and heading up Columbus so I follow.

To where they dip into Portofino Cafe where I myself take seat near back wall, wondering if I will be discovered. But there in corner table I spot Bull, baggy gray suit and black shoes, white shirt, long black thin tie, looks like those clothes went out and bought something used to put in them, sleeping on fist, and I can see from his own watch that he was supposed to be at his own reading twenty minutes ago. Then there's Urso in street, slop shoed, bare chest hair and belly hanging out black vest. He peers in but can't spot Bull in dark corner, Larry and Young Republicans at bar ordering French seltzer water so have backs turned, me, Duluoz, sequestered in back at wall hiding behind coffee cup—so don't ever try to predict what you'll be doing in twenty years, you might be dead, or worse, in a bar with old friends and still dead.

Larry sits down in his argyle sweater vest with the Young Clean Whites. They're talking to him about exhibiting his paintings in their new gallery on Union Street (right between wedding dress shop and a dildo factory). They're telling him he could use the profits from his paintings to sink back into the bookstore and publishing, publish some bright new off-Beats, besides, they'll have that dildo factory out of there soon, they got friends in city council who promised to change the zoning, and Larry with thumb under chin, two fingers on cheek and two over lips, tries to mumble something about keeping the dildo factory and there are no more Beats anymore or never were but stops and knows this ain't about Beats, never was, it's about money, one thing that Larry always knew and the rest of us didn't, which got a few tail-end hipsters in print, but did nothing for me who had to lead the way and bust tail in New York to make it possible for everybody else to exist—the tale of American art, poetry, literature is the tail of America wagging dollar dogs across the heartland, you grab somebody by the wallet ass and the head will follow and Larry knows that better than anybody—so they can hang his paintings on Union Street, good for him.

Now Urso is inside cafe and spots Hubbard, sits down says, "Hey Bull, you got to wake up, how can I play stupid if there ain't anybody smart there," and Bull open slides eyelids like deadlights, whole place turns gray under his stare; Larry looks up and sees Urso with Bull, arm slung on shoulder and the place turning grayer and darker by the second like just before the beginning of a big feature movie, everybody looking out into the darkness and nobody recognizing anybody, just the whispers of anticipation and hush before the big show begins, but there's no big show, the show's been over a long time, and when that darkness leaves Duluoz is in there by himself, a product of my own hallucinations; one thing that hasn't changed in twenty years, I'm still the worst dressed guy in the joint.

Lawrence Ferlinghetti

I've seen a thousand Kerouac imitations over the years, some better than others. But thank you for the opportunity to look at this. It's not for me, but best of luck finding a publisher.

20

Dreamed I climbed a gradual cliff from slope to slope and got up on top and sat down but suddenly in looking down I saw it was not a gradual cliff at all but sheer—in the dream no thought of getting down at all on other side—in the dream as always in High Places dreams I'm concerned with *getting down the way I came*, or rectifying my own mistakes—and even though I know it's a dream, within the dream I insist I must get down off the high cliff I climbed—the same old fear grips me in mortal throes—"But if it's a dream then the cliff is not real," I tell myself "so just wake up & the cliff will vanish"—I hardly hardly believe it's possible, and trembling, open my eyes & the dream is gone, the terror is gone—in this war of life—this flight of life has been recorded by a camera that takes pictures of people while they're crashing, you see their agony and even one shot of a man rolling over in smoke—(at the crash)—the device never breaks—We're watching a series of pictures—I am completely horrified because I identify myself and forget it's a (dream) device taking the pictures—passengers are shown in a writhing tormented assembly in the brave brown plane as it's hurling downward in the night to crash and kill them all—You see men looking at one another with expressions of intolerable regret—I watch one man looking down at the floor quietly—as the others moan and pray and writhe—He is going to allow the crash to take him quietly—But as the picture goes on, closer and closer to the actual contact moment of death as the plane nears the ground, our hero has jumped up and is shouting—No matter who you look at, the face (women, children, men) shows something never seen before on that face and never to be seen again—Intolerable regret and great bemused understanding streaked with pale slashes of fear so great I myself tormented—You see shots of the dying in smoke and flames, famous heroes in throes of agony alone not knowing their pictures are being taken or that anyone will ever see this or that anything will ever happen again—It's the loneliness of death, the selfhood of death—the fruits of self at last and the pain and terror of it—It's hold was so great, the letting go of it is a great terrified wrenching—O if I could only describe those faces, the eyes at last looking with a new, a final realization of something—Their throats gulping when they try to take it quietly, some sobbing in hands as the poor world falls screaming to destruction—O Buddha, deliver all sentient beings, live and dead.

21

In front of Bright Lights Book Store wall of Duluoz bookfaces stare out with intolerable regret, a half dozen biographies of me, letters from Irwin to Cody and back, Cody's scribbling codified in book in print, *The First Last*, and my daughter (did I have a daughter?), my daughter's book, *Road Baby*, Evelyn Pomeray's *Beatheart*, and posthumous work of me, *Visions of Dean* (the best of them all) and *Pik*, and me, posthumous Duluoz, bemused with pale slashes of fear ask myself do I come back quietly or howling? the pale oriental book clerk watches me on television from behind desk, not even needing to look up, (it's a gray blurry image like from the moon walk, a message from the moon) not needing to know if I know he is watching if this has ever happened if it will ever happen again—aah, Duluoz, you feel yourself gulping—and a book missing, *Vanity of a Hero*, I'm searching shelves of glistening Duluoz words entombed and turn my loneliness selfhood fruits to cluck, at clerk, "you got any copies of *Vanity* here?" and he says to TV screen of me (doesn't even have to look up) "it's out of print."

22

R*egard, la face de skalette dans la lune!*

23

"You need a copy? Give me your address, I'll mail it to you."

My address. But beside me is Evelyn Pomeray—(I hardly believe it's possible, but she is still there when I open my eyes)—"You'd have to send it to heaven," I say before remembering I am not even ghost of former self and have returned kindness with words of old man burdened by paradox. But it is the same dark brow dark lash Evelyn though older, thin, blonde hair up in twist.

"You'd be surprised how often I send things there," says she.

I've taken off my hat, my fatness and baldness in front of her sulking in its old fart ghostliness. "You have a book," and already my words forget themselves in that old quizzical cynical Evelyn raise of brow as she searches for my invisibilty in her memory time lost.

"And a bad movie based on it. You do your work, you let it go. Some wise guy said that a long time ago, I'm sure."

"Lao Tzu."

"His wife probably said it to him every day for ten years before he wrote it down. She lived it, he got credit for it. I'll have to go outside if I want to smoke this," cigarette which she pulls from purse, filter already propped in knuckles of hand.

Outside the moon (but not the gray and dusty moon of trodded foot) is low and gold on sky to west, white bank of fog rolling underneath like God's white beard eating sky and soon the moon and coming colder night—the moon we are denied, brown moon dream moon, poets' moon, even moon of gloom doomed lover's wish—where is Cody? the living search for him, the dead search for him, and America, searching down the torn middle of its whitebread soul, they thought they'd find him with LSD, those kids, as if you could just fly there—go back to your warm child beds alone in cold room winter night wait, your cold feet are there to remind you what waits for you while you're waiting, that cold that's coming to your heart, that real cold, lonely cold, not just the cold that makes the world cruel, but the cold like the dark new moon in fog in heart, that is who I am back in America in 1982 and my name is Death.

We can't go in the Portofino, I explain to Evelyn, because I am already too dark, and in there my brown edges disappear, so in the Cafe Roma she slips a little bourbon in our coffee as the ghostly fog rolls into the streets.

"You know the only thing I ever wanted was a house and some kids and Cody there after work, watch some TV, let Cody go up to his little room and pound out that soul of his on the typewriter."

"It was like that for a while."

"Every once in a while, for a while."

"What's outside is all a metaphor for what's inside, and you just got to go out and turn your life inside out to get at it, that's what Cody understood."

"I don't think he understood a damn thing," says she. "Too many people loved him and he couldn't say no to anybody, so all the good things made him bad. He was a simple guy turned into a cultural superman, and a myth, and a puzzle, and I just loved him for what he was and he could never figure that out because everybody else had him convinced he was so damned complex. I think about that poor bastard everyday."

"Me too."

"Well I guess a lot of people do."

"Listen, would you recognize Cody if you saw him? I mean if he was back on the street, just walking down the street, not like he looked when you last saw him, but like things had just gone on and now he was alive, just older."

"His last mistress was the very last, I'm afraid. He courted the Queen."

"You know what I think," I tell her, "that you die and just go on, nothing changes at all except you wake up somewhere else, the same person, but you have to start a new life, and the price of who you were is that you have to *stay* who you were and go on in that new life, and there are some poor fools who even have to go back and encounter everybody they used to know, whether they want to or not, and nobody recognizes them. You might be seeing Cody everyday, and he's suffering around you, meeting you, looking in your eyes, talking to you in a million excited words, you could even sleep with him and not know."

"How nice for him."

"When you die you die. When you die you go to heaven. When you die you get reincarnated as worms. It all happens. That's the thing. All of it happens. So does this."

"What."

"That you come back as yourself. It's happened to me."

"That's very interesting. I think I'm going to have to go now."

"I'm looking for Cody. And I'm not going to heaven until I find him."

"I'll give you the part about not being able to recognize you. How's that."

"I'm Jack," I tell Evelyn. "I'm Duluoz."

"Duluoz," she says breathing sigh, stops getting up, as fog from street stretches over windows in gray graveyard somber slipping through window frame and under door, as gray as Bull Hubbard's stare but colder, and the walls are gray and the people gray, Evelyn gray and gray me breathing gray fog into this crypt cafe, crypt San Francisco, and this world God made to bury bodies in—we began our rotting before God even thought it up—so I drank myself to death, the quiet final home, stay put, thought I, and wait for your Mémêre, but once again she is waiting there for me. Over shoulder in corner grayer still I hear Dr. Sax, his cane tapping through the fog.

"I think men think up a lot of crazy reasons for crawling back in the womb," says Evelyn. She lights cigarette that heats the room, orange ember raising fleshtones in her hands and face. "They do a lot of running around searching for fathers, buddies, becoming one or the other of them, or worse, Jesus or Napolean, just so their mother will love them. But they'll never be a mother, and they'll never get back in the womb, so they worship death, kill people, blow people up, brood about their own deaths while they're trying to rub out all the other boys so the Big Mother will only have one big baby boy to love. Know why I loved Cody so much? Because he had so much woman in him. That's why women loved him so much, and that's why Irwin loved him too. Cody never searched for his father. It was Duluoz who searched for Cody's father. Answer me that one. Cody worshipped life, pure and simple, like a woman, and he was all man, more man than anybody, more than Jack, that's why Jack worshipped him too. Look at *Visions*. For a while he was more obsessed with Cody than he was himself."

"I loved Cody more than anyone."

"Maybe you're not Duluoz. Maybe you just think you are. You wouldn't be the first. It makes as much sense as your theory about coming back as yourself."

Yeah, but if that's true, would I have written this?

Aaah phooey!

Carolyn Cassady

Give me a break.

24

Me: Why does anybody write anything down?

Self: If no reason on earth, what more reason in heaven?

Me: Because any time you sit down and put words on the page, that's where you are and that's where you want to stay.

Self: So where did I go when I went home to write this book?

Me: Who knows what novel lurks in the heart?

Self: The Shadow knows (Wa-ha-ha-ha-ha!).

25

Back in Mission I get bus ticket to New York. A dead man in land's end, I'm not going to stop in Denver to shoot pool, not in Lawrence to shoot Hubbard (he probably wouldn't be there anyway), just ride this silver busoleum straight to New York, catch the first thing on wheels to Boston and Lowell and find some way to crawl into my grave.

"The only problem with that is you'll have a hard time finding it."

It's my old friend the Indian bum with key chain flag of Mexico and Our Lady of Guadelupe.

"I must have been talking out loud," I say as bus leaves station, all the time thinking how I wheedled my way into this very last back seat on bus, telling attendant I had bad back and bad kidneys so I could get on first and be alone near the toilet with no window so I could practice being alone in the dark.

"It's poorly marked," says he.

"You think I'd have trouble finding my own grave?"

"Have you been there before?"

"In a manner of speaking. I was practically born there."

"It's hard to find. Just a flat stone, grass growing over it. No directions."

"You know a lot about my grave in Lowell, Massachusetts for an old Indian."

"Maybe I just look like an old Indian. Look at you, you look like you're alive."

"Either that or I just don't feel like life anymore."

"Now you're getting profoondified. To have seen the spectre isn't everything, and there are deathmasks piled, one atop the other, clear to heaven. Commoner still are the wan visages of those returning from the shadow of the valley. This means little to those who have not lifted the veil."

It was at this point, if I'd had a brain in my head of death, than I'd have known where I was headed and why I was going, but I didn't, so why tell you what I already know because I didn't know it then (a lesson to those of you who always found old Duluoz so wrapped up in his over-romantic and immediate present that he didn't know the difference between person and page—the difference between a dummy and a genius is that some people are too dumb to tell the difference —), as it was I was apprehensive, I didn't want to ride all the way to New York with this old Indian chattering profoondities and shifting diction, I was worried I'd find a way back into my grave and I'd turn around and he'd be in there blubbering with me! following the normal laws of doom!

That hurricane afternoon began clearly enough with the sudden riptide pace of thin snaveled clouds across the glary pale above; to add to all that horror, of old chattering Indian ghost and clouds racing so fast that you didn't quite believe it and looked twice like a comedian in a B-movie, a doubletake; a sinister whirlwind metaphor afternoon where as we left the freeway to pick up passengers in little cowtown California valley Davis a telephone pole caught fire and fell on the bus! Everybody piling out like burnt match sticks! You've got to read your omens, it was time to take a walk.

And not a couple hundred yards from there sitting in baking valley California sun is one of them California U-nee-versities, old fig trees growing here and there in patches amid cement, little plaques on them say "these are the original fig trees that grew here when this was the old Davis farm after which this university and town were named," making you wonder of course why they kept these particular fig trees and put plaques on them, bulldozed everything else. Out beyond fig trees is large grassy square filled with studentry lazing on grass, playing catch with plastic discs (not a football in sight), everywhere blond young youngblonds bustling buzzily about on bicycles with nylon versions of old rucksacks across backs, everywhere you look seas of parked bicycles. It's too much blond young! Too much white wine quiche happiness! Old Duluoz feels like H.G. Wells' character among the Eloi. Where's the factories? I'm just about to head back where I came, brave the smoking bus and Desno telephone poles (get out of town before Morlocks come out of manholes to eat us) when out corner of eye spot poster that says POETRY READING

TODAY BY FAMOUS BEAT POET JAPHY RYDER—so Raphael was right, Japhy is teaching at a riding school, only I thought it was horse riding school and here it's bike riding school.

Japhy reads in little auditorium, looks like it seats about two hundred and is half full, mostly long hair types, a few grizzly old profs and some fat doughy man in front row drinking from brown paper bag. Japhy's wearing a suit, an old baggy job, sad white shirt and thin tie, looks like the same suit of clothes that went to the Salvation Army and found Hubbard; wispy youth beard now wispy old beard, eyes crinkled in gentle China smile, face wrinkled more than suit, saying something about voting, vote for the Earth, our Mother, not much poetry, Japhy says voting is more important than poetry and I can see by his simple lip grin he's just telling them an old Buddhist lie that's better than the truth, decrying that old Buddhist problem, the problem with words, try as you might they fall into sentences and before you know it you mean something or they do or somebody does (who cares?) (everybody of course!).

Japhy finishes up to mild applause, doughman gets up, short black mustache dwarfed in flesh of face, puts arm around Japhy and invites everybody to his house for drinks with poet. Outside everybody mounting fancy shiny bicycles with more gears than an eighteen wheeler, a small hornet nest of Japhy loving bicyclist aficionados pedaling off to doughman's for cocktails, only thing to do is find friendly unchained fat tired gearless bike, city probably provides them at these kinds of events in case you forgot the combination to your lock and need to go somewhere, send truck out in the morning and collect them all up like grocery carts, either that or God, author of all fate (we don't choose our suffering we just choose our sins) has left one for Duluoz.

It's a grand fat little cowtown with sun seeping down into hot evening, everybody on their porches eating crepes discussing whether or not to take out equity loan to put a spa on the veranda, an eight foot stone wall around the graveyard so all you can see is the tops of the palm trees and that should tell you something, kind of place where they only bury people on the day between Wednesday and Thursday, tan bike police in khaki shorts waiting on corners to arrest you for wandering outside bike lane in fact get a friendly visitation from one as I puff along, reminding me that dusk is approaching and I don't have a light on my bicycle so best I get where I'm going and stay there by sunset (or get thrown down manhole to spend rest of Time under earth with old gray Morlocks, making bicycles!).

I stop at driveway with a hundred new bikes piled in magnificent quiet orderly array, chrome shining wheels in streetlights, take walk around block to make sure to avoid late arrivals, then go to window where inside the doughman moves with drink amidst co-eds, speaking in lip cur lift of lip, eyebrows browing, drink moving in fingers like fire baton at half-time of football game—he followed by tall gangly blonde girl who puts him in half-nelson like old TV wrestler and drags him away till he can break loose and move back to center ring, throw flying drop kick; off to side is old white-haired kindfaced (must be) poet, spectacle eyed in spectacles bespectacling the room in quiet "I seen it all before" and remembering when he was the Japhy Ryder (and more!) of anemic academe and said "ah yes, Auden, a few good poems, but so burly with his wordly words," or some such as students surround him write it down in minds to reiterate in cafeterias and student coffee shops—wordly burls of Auden, is that it? no, worldly birds, birdy words, whirly birds progenerated into student poems ala Proofrock when they themselves recreate cocktail parties, all that's left for poets these days—

At end of room Japhy sits Buddha-eyed in straight chair, young poets in poetic procession handing him sheets of poems, Japhy reads, nods, smiles, girl with long brown hair and fingers that write poems about playing the piano in rooms filled with Impressionist paintings, you can tell, those fingers are long and white and dancing as Japhy smiles at her poem, her shoulders, her feet, are playing the piano—do you think I can send it to the *New Yorker*? she asks him—Yes, he says—the *Atlantic*?—Yes, he says, send it—she's written a short story she tells him, about a young housewife who one day steps into her yard and turns into a tree—Japhy is nodding, thinking yes, send it, to the Governor, the President, fill the world with poems, poems your mother taught you before you knew what a poem was (or thought you knew what it was supposed to be). Japhy sips his red wine, holds it between lips and teeth, swallows, eyes narrow—down from the mountain, drunk with a different kind of butchers.

26

"Who's this?"

"Who's what?"

"He's not hurting anybody, just sleeping under a bush."

"Well everybody's gone. Maybe he's hurt. We should do something. We should call the police." It's the gangly blonde.

"Last time I called the police they arrested me," says doughman.

"Because you threw all the furniture out the front window!"

"My yard. My furniture."

I'm on back on lawn and just regaining focus, doughman and gangly blonde with feet at my head, faces up in the air and upside down.

"Well we have to do something," says she.

"I'm not a Morlock," I say.

"He has an informed world view," says Doughman tipping iceglass into face. "I can't call the authorities on somebody with a *weltenschuang*."

"No welt on my schlong," I say. "I'm a Wangerian Reductionist."

"I didn't know Wagner had a world view," says blonde.

"Are you kidding?" says doughman. "I didn't know he had a welt on his schlong."

"Not Wagner, *wanger*. I reduce everything to my wanger."

"Oh, I thought it was something new," says he.

"Old as death."

"I think we should call somebody," she says.

"It's okay," I hear Japhy say from my feet. He offers me his hand. "I'll drop him off where he wants to go on my way home."

Japhy drives a little truck, a Chevrolet, and looks fine at the wheel with his crumpled suit slipping out of flat mild Davis CA and into shadow hills under white coyote moon; for a moment we are on strip of freeway lines bejeweled by reflectors on black asphalt and roadside disappears, black road ahead disappears in sky, road jewels stretch to stars of star road jeweled sky—we are driving in stars—and then the hills in the shadow of moon, warm arm hills holding their roads—if you fall asleep at the wheel and drive into the salt flats around Salt Lake you'll wake up an hour later still driving, but these hills would give you a blanket and put you to sleep with warm cows muttering (mothering) your forehead—truck alights on wind road, headlights, Japhy driving like deer, calm and perked on this road of intrusion, the animals around, he says, have generations on generations of racial memories without roads, like the moths and fire, and where do roads fit in with their sad necessity? ah, humanity, with your machines and roads like sword of Zen Master cutting the arguing bikhus' cat in two (even King Solomon of old Israel only *threatened* to split that baby, didn't actually do it), this is what happens when you own something (and longtime difference between yours truly and Japhy—while I mourned for mouse on Desolation, killed him because he ate my food, mouse who looked at me at moment of death with pain of all sentient things, with eyes of Christ, Japhy could live with mouse forever, let him die of old age in flour sack, or even break his neck with thump of thumb, all the same gentle Zen lunacy) (actually difference between Zen Buddhist and Catholic Buddhist) (other small differences too, like attitude toward drinking)—so get in your car and drive home like everybody else!

"Japhy," I say, "are you Buddha down there with the hackademics?"

Japhy turns wheel and truck leans at winding edge, glimpse of yellow moon spilled silver valley, farm squares, ranch house light beam, road spread, river split, shadows of cloud drift moonlight.

"It's even more simple," says Japhy. "They love poems."

"Oh baaa, they think they love poems but just want to ride academic coattail to cooshy semi-fame, teach college, get laid."

"By the way, let me know where you want to get off."

"You can't get out of a moving truck on a mountain, it's an old Zen saying."

"There was somebody there who wanted to do his dissertation on you, Jack."

"What makes you think I'm me. Nobody else seems to think I'm me."

"They even let him do it."

"Oh yeah, what he say?"

"He quit and moved to Utah."

"Serves him right."

"Said he'd rather write novels."

"He should forget it, it's a lost art. I'll probably have to write one more just to remind everybody."

"That's a wonderful idea, Jack," says Japhy all twinkle eyed in dashboard and moonlight, "it's been a while since you've published anything, maybe you can get it excerpted in the *New Yorker*."

Well who would've remembered that Japhy was funny, all those serious earth poems, loving rocks and fish and cold water.

"Aah, the *New Yorker* was begging me for stuff, I only turned them down so I wouldn't embarrass you and Irwin who wanted to get in there so bad."

"Well I might take a job at Davis some time soon," says Japhy. "I need the money."

"Well simple me that," says I.

27

Japhy is a dawn riser moreso than ever now that age is upon him and the days narrowing like thin streaks of light between the nights, though there's no rush or franticness, just more concentration as he makes his tea, splits his wood, pets his goat, stares at the wind around the trees. He's got half his day over before I even wake up, sore as a board, and eat some kind of breakfast flaffel with my tea. Right now he's alone—his wife, God bless, is not there—up here somewhere in some foothills keeping things simple, got topographical maps of the whole area marked with water tables and watersheds and weather records and charts, files of correspondence to *congresspeople* (that's what it says on file, Duluoz would never use such an ugly word, but there's Japhy once again with his sword of politics splitting aesthetical cats) and senators and file clerks and presidents, he is Zen Emerson keeping it clean where he squats, though he himself doesn't use the word *Zen* anymore, he sometimes uses the word *practice* in the terminal sense because he's not practicing for anything and there isn't anything he practices or gets better at, this all coming out in conversation over tea and beans and nights on porch farting under star cold air sipping light plum wine, matching night calls of owl cricket coyote with anal hoot biological haiku, everything recycling up here in perfect rhythm charted by Japhy—what needs nitrogen when—we piss around cabin in Zodiacal arcs, shit in rhythm with bears, even have designated areas to beat off, none of which is premeditated but generated by natural tendencies anyway, if you just went around up here and did what you wanted, says Japhy, you'd find yourself in the same arc, same patterns, same rhythms, pissing and shitting and beating off in the same places, marking your territory, recycling, purifying, clearing out dead patches of wood so new things can grow, everything in balance, even death, the non-being that balances being, equally necessary, that's why, he figures, I'm back, at least in the general sense, though specifically why I'm back he doesn't know and neither do I; there was a while I thought I'd been living in Mexico but now I'm not so sure, old Memory Babe Duluoz can't even remember Mexico now, now I feel like I woke up on that bus to Juarez next to that Mexican Indian with the key chain.

"I think you're born relaxed or you're not," I tell Japhy. "Some people are born into hectic Chinese food lunch huz-buz martini life, or work-a-day beer bar life, raise a million kids and die life, not everybody gets educated in Berkeley and Japan and gets money to live on mountain top by writing neo-haiku."

"Some people don't know anything, and they're proud of it," says Japhy.

"I'm just saying that you get lived through by something and I don't know what, and if you don't take responsibility you don't get anywhere, and when you do you're wrong and it's sad. Just when you think you're free of yourself, your self gets plopped right back on you."

"The souls of suicides wander the earth," says Japhy. "It's a strange thing, because first, there is no-soul, and second, suicide is the most rational act of all. But then again, there's nothing on this side of life, or the other, that is rational."

"Japhy, this ain't a book, we don't have to talk silly oblique dialogue like Hemingway. Talk to me. You're saying I'm a ghost."

"Well, we're all ghosts."

"I died of natural self-destructive causes."

"You've got to find something, and it's not me."

"Maybe it is you."

"Okay, maybe it is."

"Phooey, you belong down there teaching bike riding."

"That hasn't stopped me from doing it."

"Ah Japhy, quit being so smart."

But it's still mountain heaven and unlike Japhy who can sit and watch the sun go down, I watch the sunset for a minute and the thought of it ending makes me want to leave, worse, I get my fill of beauty and then who needs more, it must be time to eat or something else, that's probably why I'm back, I got bored with death and all its silent black gloominess and needed to do something.

Japhy can sense it and in the morning he's got packs packed and plans planned, hats out, walking sticks lined up at door. I've been there two weeks and though it only feels like I've been there a day I'm tired of it already and Japhy's going to take me on a hike to the top of something before driving me down to the valley and putting me back on the bus. Looks like even Japhy can get too much of a good thing.

"Where?" says I.

"Top of the World."

Sounds like a long hike for old men and besides I thought Top of the World would be somewhere in Tibet. But the Top of the World is anywhere everywhere as we all well know. If you want to find somewhere that isn't you have to dig a hole and even then, relatively speaking, you're still pretty close to the top, just a little underneath.

"Okay let's go, which direction."

"Get in the truck," says Japhy.

We end up taking a long ride, spending a lot of time on back roads in the flatlands through tomato fields (poor Mexican families sweating under sun, nothing changed in forty years) then Japhy finally turns off on dirt road and begins climb up mountain, winding back and forth, kids on tall skinny-tire motorcycles whining by on right and left up and down, occasional pick-up trucks pulled off to side with teen-agers drinking beer and smoking pot and cigarettes, girls with heads tucked under boy arm, teen-age redneck love, future babies and divorces marriages and abortions, sad future of adulthood strewn all over that dirt road on the way to the Top of the World (what happened to good old cheerleading and football? Sunday afternoons of baseball hayfield soda pop? this probably some national trend of youth, and somebody writing for Time Magazine doing his socio-popology and blaming all this on me like they did the Hippies).

It's a long enough ride but eventually Japhy stops, parking in little make-shift parking lot with crowd of motorbikes and pick-up trucks and hot rods, just above us huge towers surrounded at the bottom with cyclone fence topped with barbed wire, lots of signs everywhere saying to stay away, nobody should be up there. On top the towers are huge concave discs with antennae pointing out the middle at the sky. There's teen-agers everywhere on blankets necking, drinking beer and wine, smoking, throwing bottles and cans into that same blue sky those antennae point in.

"C'mon," says Japhy and we get the packs and hats and walking sticks out of the back of the truck and I follow him up past several towers to the one that sits at the very top of the mountain; teen-age hoods on motorcylces whine up and circle us a few times, spinning out back tires toward cliff edge and throwing wine bottles at last second as they plant foot and race back to the towers. Sky all around us. And to the east you can see the whole valley stretching out flat like a quilt under an airplane, Sacramento and American Rivers twisting into gleam of silver buildings rising out of the flats, old Sacramento like Oz, and all around the other towns of the county, Davis and the Mexican farm towns, Woodland, Dixon, Winters, Vacaville (in Spanish, cowtown), Yuba City (with football team named after geese, called Honkers), Knight's Landing (where there's a an old hunter's bar called Dutch Miller's, a monument to death with a million kinds of dead stuffed animals inside and Dutch in there serving up drinks and free sandwiches, old Dutch, bald, toothcrooked, got a tie with a palm tree and bathing beauty on it that lights up, his son behind the bar with hook for hand, lost that hand in Vietnam War, sign out front in neon misspelled and never replaced says "Duth's") and just south of there the sprawling Delta where the roads run parallel to little rivulets and you have to take small ferries to get from town to town, isolated communities of Swedes and Chinese and Japanese and Dutch misanthropists, and then you can look west over the Coastal Range and Rumsey Canyon with it's Esparto and Guinda and almonds (which they all pronounce like salmon over there) all the way to Vallejo and the Carquinez Straight, the Suisun Bay and the San Pablo Bay, the edge of the City dropping to the water at the edge of the San Francisco Bay and the Pacific Ocean, and the Golden Gate stretching across to Marin; it's an amazing sight and you can see everything in Northern California with a turn of the head; you can see your memories from a distance, you can see lives.

"What kind of towers are these?" I ask Japhy.

"Microwave towers," he says. "They're for television."

"Okay," says I, "let's go."

"No place to go," says giggling Japhy Ryder, "this is it."

This is it. We are two old coots in floppy hats and packs with walking sticks on top a TV tower mountain surrounded by mean teen-agers with pick-ups and motorcycles while around us the disinformation of the planet rages in or out (who knows?) silently in waves. We're all trespassing. We all have a nice view!

Then there's a loud whine of engine behind us followed by teen-age blood scream as motorcyclist leans back on bike and stands up on back wheel, yells of screaming kids in air drowning fanfare, cans and bottles fly like confetti as motorcycle flies over small bumps, comes down on front tire, goes up again coming right toward us! and me and Japhy step aside just in time as bike hits edge of cliff, we can see face of teen-age doom beneath insect goggles and crash helmet, teeth of skeleton and red gumlust of mad child in sex death machine dance frenzy as bike flies into air, then moment of calm desperate realization as motorcycle and rider disappear over cliff edge into space below.

Then before I can even look back for double-take, another biker is up on back wheel and circling, lapping the wheel of bumps, arm raised in crazy exuberance of fist inside arc of bottles and cans, a tunnel of ferocious screams before hitting edge of cliff and taking mad flight dive. It happens again and again! Is this why Japhy has brought me? to witness new boyteen death ritual? I see Putsy Keriakopoulus in the air on bike, Iddyboy and Al Didier, Orestas and Telemachus Gringas and Christy Kelakis, Artaud, Rigas, McFee. G.J., the whole Lowell High football team with heads of skeletons and knocking bones lines up on motorcycles and races to air searing death plunge. I realize then that Japhy *did* bring me here to see this circle of death—look! look! how we find our deaths in moment we are eternal/young, we leap forward and write DEATH in sky with wheels, that Dr. Sax in his goodly darkness lied to us all (his best gentle lie), and when our own snakes under guise of eating evil in their natural way, in their love, make the babies of the earth, this is what we offer them, the choice of death before we become ourselves and bring our children to this cliff—Japhy, impassive, watches this sky writing with calmness of sage looking back at present as if it happened years ago, look of knowledge and regret and relief.

So it is Duluoz who scrambles over hill in vain (com)passion and disbelief to find wreckage, bikes and bodies in terminal moment of broken glide, thinking of the long last moments in air, engine revving between thighs, raining noise and life into air on way to death. But instead I see them all there hanging in daylight, wheels cocked and raised, a dozen boys in flight on their machines, fists raised, and waiting.

28

I find them all down at the bottom of the hill, helmets off, bikes in disarray, hanging out and laughing and drinking beer and eating sandwiches, girlfriends draped over shoulders like love-sacks. One of them, the biggest and strongest, the leader, looks a little older, twenty maybe, his arms bulging out of his T-shirt, sleeves rolled, dark hair combed back, he smokes a cigarette and looks up at me from arms of draping blonde, looks up with lightning eyes of all immortal youth, Top of the World Adonis. Then for just a moment he looks small old with grizzled whitened beard. Something glistens brownly from his belt, hangs from his belt and there's a moment when I see a wave of red and green, a brown Madonna without child, and then he points skyward with beer in hand to pale effigy moon in pale blue light, nobone halfbanana moonsloping in that once tangled sky. He's just a kid. He points to me and then back at the moon. "I'm going home," he yells. "Going home."

29

"So Japhy," I'm saying on last night under mountain stars on his little porch, plum wined and drowsy and body warm under Mexican blanket on steps, Japhy himself folded in rocking chair in blanket under pancho and sweater, arms tucked, pancho tucked, blanket tucked, folded in folds, disappearing under soft rag of clothes of cotton, wool, got himself in some kind of cocoon folded from inside out, making me wonder how he could get all folded up like that so precisely and still have his hands on the inside until one slips out to ceramic cup on railing for wine and raises it to lips, then places it back down on railing again and disappears under wrapping, faint thin hand like smoke, like some ghost hand, not Japhy's hand at all, just something summoned up for sip of wine, "I'm too old to know there's a point to anything."

Japhy smiles his whimsy smile like imp—delicacy and precision beneath his layers of ragamuff, his very own personified layers of opposites, which he pretty much says himself right next—"All I've ever learned," says Japhy Ryder "is to speak each syllable as if it were a pebble. That articulate and small, and round, or edged, divoted, gray, or spotted, or smooth. And that simple. And understand that it is a mountain. And how small a mountain is."

"And how small is that?"

"As small as it is."

"That's easy for you to say," I tell Japhy—too much time sitting and breathing and collapsing relatives and absolutes into each other, then kaboom! nothin left—"but everything's still there, you've still got to make your mark on the world, or not!"

"Or not," says Japhy. "Listen Jack, what good did it do you to join the world of official literature. People hated you, your best books rotted, you hated yourself, your gentleness was squeezed into suffering."

"I'd've suffered anyways. I was born to suffer."

"Well part of you believed in the literary meritocracy."

"Tell me about it, Mr. *Norton Anthology*."

"The real history, the real literature, most of it is never found."

"Or written, ha!"

"It's been written."

"Hey, who hated me anyway?"

"There are times I regret being drawn in. I've told myself that if I can't come down from the mountain, then I have not been on the mountain, that I must be on the mountain, even when I am not on the mountain."

"There you go again."

"Wait Jack. Think about who we are, not just you and me, but all of us, and what we did, what anyone would have to know to understand us, all that Buddhist, Existentialist, Judeo, Catholic, trans-American, trans-Atlantic, trans-Pacific, pan-cultural stuff. We were almost reactionary, and we spawned reactionaries, in the best sense, people who wanted to clean things up with their hearts, to plant things, experience things first hand without the mediation of technological culture. So what have people read? Howling. Road. Getting Married. They skim from the gleaning with cursory glances. Often I think that I'm lucky, and you're unfortunate, because *Road* will be read, misinterpreted, loved, vilified in the next century, and maybe the next."

"Baloney!"

"To quote an old friend, from an old book."

"You're giving me the baloney sutra."

"Well Jack, then you tell me why you're back? What's going to be different this time?"

"Okay," I say, "you remember back then around the same time—I wrote about it in *Buddha Bums*—when those little kids came around throwing rocks on our shack roof? Remember?"

"Yes."

"One afternoon at the time when you and I had a little jet-black cat, they came sneaking to the door to look in. Just as they were about to open the door I opened it, with the black cat in my arms, and said in a low voice, 'I am the ghost.' They gulped and looked at me and believed me and said, 'Yeah.' Pretty soon they were over the other side of the hill. They never came around throwing rocks again."

"We think we live in our bodies, but we don't."

"No, they just didn't ever come back throwing rocks."

"Jack," says Japhy, "you left, the kids came back."

"They did?"

"Yes."

"Well okay, who cares."

"You?"

"Maybe me."

"Jack, it was good to see you again," says Japhy, but by now his whole self is like that wispy hand, something under panchos and blankets that gets things done but isn't there.

30

This whole episode being a parable for all you rock throwers out there who think Duluoz didn't know the meaning of unreliable narration or narrative distance (in time or space) (as if any rock thrower ever did). Remember this. There's never more complexity or big am*big*uity or irony or paradox or contradiction than in the just plain truth. Aah, why do I bother(?) (answer that yourself).

Gary Snyder

Something I always argued about with Jack was the blank spaces. He believed everything he wrote was true, which you might think a naive view of language, but it was true like a spontaneous jazz riff. Jack was no dummy. He came at everything from the other side without telling anyone he'd bothered to circumvent. He knew what people wanted a writer to be. Then he forgot. Sometimes on purpose, sometimes not. That was the beauty. And, of course, part of what killed him.

But when you write something down, even "true" things, you select. Leave things out. Jack spent two weeks with me. But there aren't two weeks of words, or events, in the above passage. The blank spaces are true, too. Even more true.

As I said, we argued about these things. Not seriously, but seriously. Not heated, but engaged, playful. Jack had read his Joyce and Proust. Tolstoy and Dostoyevsky. He knew about the people who tried to fill all the gaps. And he knew the people who played with them, like Hemingway. Me, even. He did not read Nargajuna, or the schools that followed him, monks doing language game things like, say, the followers of Wittgenstein, but we talked about it, because Jack really did try to understand the roots of Zen, which, as you know, he rejected. He called himself an old fashioned Hinayana bikkhu, but he was more Theravadin than anything, at least when he practiced. Being Catholic. Really. That kind of root thinking. He could no more practice Zen than Protestantism. So there's all that playful stuff in *Dharma Bums*. Zen lunacy. Which, as you probably know, he quotes from there at the end. The episode about the cat and ghost. The parable. Making it all rather parabolic, even meta-parabolic. And I mean all the puns. And so did he.

It wouldn't be beyond Jack to read J. Hillis Miller. Think it was bunk. Then employ the strategy. And never let anyone know. That's the point about the rock throwers. Critics. Editors even. Jack was wrong about a lot of things, in terms of what he thought America expected of its writers. Truth was one of those mistakes. But he knew that the publishing establishment did not want intellectuals. Intellectuals are not good story tellers. Aren't entertaining. Of course, enough intellectuals find something interesting and you can sell to them. But Jack was an anti-intellectual intellectual. He believed in sentiment and ideas. The *true* things. One alienated him from the entertainment industry, the other from the academy.

Such a capacity to bring words together in unexpected, beautiful ways. Spontaneous co-originating language. And to do it in prose.

He had a remarkable memory. Still does.

So, yes, Jack Kerouac is dead. I'm also very glad he came back. It was good to see him, though I really don't remember doing so. In fact, I don't recall any of the above story at all.

31

Bus ride to New York. I finished *Road* more or less in '51 though I'd been working on it for a long time in a lot of ways long before that, versions not titled *Road*, versions in my head, lots of versions before I finally sat down and got it all out on teletype paper, spontaneous and immediate like all good writing; and then, in '51, I was only around thirty and when you're thirty you're just a guy in your twenties who turned thirty, still a young man, and that's the truth about *Road*, it's a youthful book, sad in its optimism, (over fuddled with and oversimplified by editors and thus made to look more naive than it was really) and most anybody in America who's gone to college and eaten a hot dog (both) has read it and knows it didn't get in print till '57 and that when I became a youthful cultural hero I wasn't youthful anymore, I had the better part of my thirties behind me and thinking about forty and that's the time in life when your bones ache everyday even when you're not sick, you never get through a night without having to get up and piss and the last time you slept the blank dreamless sleep of God is just a dream itself, your life is better than half over and you know too many dead people already, and you try to remember the last pure moment when you ate up great moments of life in gulps and the past in its brownness was soft and kind and the future something that would happen to *you*, you in your valuable madness which should all be recorded, Proust-like, on tape if not on paper because there's just too much of it; well, something happens, you're just plain tired all the time; back in '51 I might have been dying but my cells still remembered being alive and by the end of the decade the last thing any of me remembered was being tired, and that's when drunkenness turns from Dionysian reverie to die on your knees and memory, you just want to kill enough things in your mind so you can sleep, death looks more scary and more welcome all the time and you wake up at night in sweat (from booze nerves from same booze that put you to sleep) remembering the future of Death, also the pervading moodiness of life is sorrow and sadness which you see everywhere and can't escape or help and there are moments when you forget it but that's all, just a few moments.

Getting famous (and loved and hated) didn't change any of that, in fact, following the normal course of human absurdity you get famous for the wrong things. None of it changed where I was headed. And neither did getting off that bus in Davis and seeing Japhy. In both cases I fell like rainwater and went. It happened, (I wrote it down), it speaks for itself, for me as well as you, which is the point of this book. I just got back on the bus (still waiting there in afternoon light like bus I'd left two weeks before, only no burnt telephone pole and no Mexican Indian sharing back seat) and rode to New York.

Now I sat down flashing out this last book determined not to do what it might look like I'm doing here, that's straighten everybody out about what I did before, but this is the bus ride from one coast to another and you probably think I had a lot of time to think back there in dark corner of bus, Sacramento, Reno, Salt Lake City, Little America Wyoming and Cheyenne, (across the Continental Divide—where all the water goes one way or the other to one ocean or the other—I, Duluoz, crossed it again for the last time, and all I'm doing here is standing on top of the mountain and *pointing it out*—old Hozomeen never looked so good—Words...The stars are words...Who succeeded? Who Failed?—the Bottomless Horror is words—you see the fire or you don't), Lincoln, Omaha, Des Moines, Iowa City, Youngstown, Hazleton, Newark, New York. There.

32

Out of Hell's Kitchen I get a cab down to the Village where unfortunately, even there, people are dressing better. I get lost among the drug dealers and dildo shops around Washington Square, stop to watch little Negro kids skidding around doing wild flailing acrobatics to bee-bop on sheets of cardboard on street. I pitter around in new chic silk suit So Ho, art galleries fancy bars—ain't nobody living here no more that ain't got no money—not an artist in the bunch—they all moved somewhere (Emeryville they told me in San Francisco) (here they're probably across the river in one room flats in Hoboken, or Brooklyn lofts) (in So Ho you have to apply for an apartment—man tells me in marble brass bar where I pay $7.50 for a drink—by showing slides of paintings—I think of poet taking slides of poems, huge sprawling epics of thousand words to page ((so to equal a picture!)), "let me in! my drivel drabbles as good as paint! I'll sell these for a dollar each! make millions! pay rent!" wonder if that's why Larry switched to painting).

I'm ruck-sack sack sucked in So Ho. Shoulda just caught the bus to Boston. But why am I leading myself on? Coulda skipped New York, too, but have urge to find bottle of cheap tokay and wander down to Bowery and sit with some human beings, only thing stopping me is that I'm afraid I'll run into that Indian, stymie me timbers! when out from art gallery comes Tom Saybrook, author of Gone! (first book on Beats for which he feared I harbored resentment of him for years, which was only true in terms of the resentment, *Gone!* was a fine novel if you wanted a look at the Beats from the outside and intellectual young man in crisis perspective, like some smart guy going into the jungle with Marlow and writing the book on Kurtz—oh-oh, shouldn't of brought the wife!—of course back then that's what all those crackerjacks in publishing right here in New York wanted, perspective, wanted you to be goddamn Truman Capote—is he dead yet?— anyway Tom was a great friend but for all his preaching to me about drinking, in fact at the end he wouldn't come over anymore, wouldn't even talk to me on the phone—"Have you been drinking Jack?" "Of course not, Tom." "You sound like you've been drinking." "If you don't want to come down, Tom, just don't fucking come down. Don't give me this 'you been drinking.'" "Well Jack, I just don't want to go through the same things over and over." Like I wasn't any *fun*). Tom looks like aging Wall Street Tweedle Dum professor, hair greased and black glasses tweed sport coat white shirt, not a thing about him changed except his body which is now rounder than mine; those glasses look like something perched independently on his head like a noseless bird borrowing eyes; in fact we might even knock heads but bellies get there first as we bounce off each other, eyes meet, and I'll tell you right now that what I see around him is the halo of pale ghostliness, privileged vision of the once dead is you can see the ghost of someone who's near dying, it sits around them like mist off ice, and it's a sad thing, even if you've come back, like me, because you're not who you were, not to anybody else, you just don't know what's going to happen—if I'm dead, where's Mémêre? Emile? Gerard? Cody? (is he dead? really? can Cody die?)—I didn't feel it myself, in those last days; what I felt was cold, in my hands, my feet; I felt something leaving but it was more like the heat off a muffin.

"Can I help you?" says Tom.

Good old Tom, first thing he wants to do is help. He reaches in his coat for pipe, packs tobacco, lights, draws, eyes squinting in that street light, all I can stammer is "How do you feel?"

"Do I know you?"

"Years ago," I say. "Some of those big parties."

"Well the kids still do it," says he. "Go to clubs. All the jewelry and make-up. It's very different now."

"Sure is!"

"Punks. Heavy Metal. Glam. What strange words."

Tom still talking words, like he could get a grip on it all with them, get the words and write a book.

"They're afraid of Death!" I say.

"Who isn't?"

"But they're so young."

"Scary world now," says Tom. "Air, food, water, sex, electrical power, everything we were brought up with, all the symbols of warmth and nourishment, now they kill as much as the atom bomb, more. So every night is Halloween."

Tom in ghost aura talking Halloween to the unrecognized dead. Who ever needs to write a thing?

"Just in town for the night," I say. "Anybody reading poetry anywhere anymore?"

"Wouldn't know," says Tom, "but Alyce Newman is inside," says pointing inside gallery, "she's pretty in touch with the literary scene here. I just come down from Connecticut every once in a while, look at paintings."

"Seen any of Larry O'Hara's?"

"Ah well," says Tom smiling. He wanders off, ghost following.

From doorway I recognize Alyce Newman, roundfaced and droop eyed under hair still straightflat thin, under that smart day to day resignation of hers, that real life savvy of work-a-day dense common sense, too full of real feel, meaning, communication (ah, but she has sadness, she still has sadness, and that's what I recognized in that girl of twenty-five years ago when she thought she could darn socks into man's heart) (and almost did!)—there she is with brown of memory everywhere about her—I'm waving to her because penguin doorman won't let me in without invitation. "Let him in," she says, "he's with me."

"You recognized me," I say once inside.

"No, I just don't think someone who's trying to get into an art gallery should be kept out, besides, you made eye contact."

"Aah yaass," I say W.C. Fields-like, "a desire for art in eyes. Dangeroos."

"Should I recognize you?"

"Who painted all these cakes?"

"That man over there, the thin one. He's Californian."

"A Californian who paints cakes."

"I edited some books about him."

"Cakes! Only cakes!"

"It has more to do with color, planes of color, color fields, I'm sure you know these things."

"Aah yaass, an editor," I say.

"And you know something about editors."

"Known a few in my day." And I'm thinking just then how editors, be they male or female, are like wives, marrying you for your potential and thinking of all they'll get changed before they put you out there on the street, make you get job, wear suit, meet relatives, talk in nice complete sentences everyone will understand, then end up fighting with you about everything and briefly accepting the slob you are, watching sad decline in front of world, your failure for not listening, then leave you for somebody else. The only good editor is your mother!

"Well I'm sure you'll be all right here on your own," says Alyce.

"But you won't mind if I just follow you around?"

"You're a little old for me."

But I follow her around anyways, looking at paintings of pastel cakes, trying to remember if Alyce was always so sad, so round, round sadness, movement of hip sadness, thin ankle in heels sadness, her getting up for work in mourning, my breakfast, coffee waiting, what kind of life would that have been with our lugging our middle aged roundness around now, she the smart editor, me dead, or worse, not, I'm struck suddenly in moment of old fear, as if everybody in room is some woman I have known.

"Tom Saybrook said you'd know if anybody was reading poetry anywhere in the Village tonight," I finally say, tired of looking at cakes, myself all caked with memory fear.

"You know Tom?"

"Years ago. Knew that whole crowd."

"Jan Duluoz is reading down at the Cornelia Street Cafe."

"Duluoz," I say.

"Daughter," says she. "Laura's kid."

"Her name isn't Jan."

"I guess you did know that crowd."

"Not Duluoz either."

"Give her a break. She can call herself anything she wants. If I wanted to call myself Duluoz, who cares? Johnnie uses Duluoz when it suits her."

"Johnnie got married."

"So did Laura."

"Johnnie goes by Duluoz?"

"What, you missed the funeral? Half the women were named Duluoz."

"Not you."

"I didn't marry him."

"You can't just take somebody's name."

"He *gave* it to Jan.

"Says who?"

"Jan."

"Her name's Mickey."

"She was his daughter. He told her she could use his name. It's common knowledge. If she wants to change her first name that's her business too."

"She's doing it to sell books."

"That poor girl is Duluoz's daughter. He never did a thing for her."

A roundfaced girl with black hair comes to see me in Lowell. A thousand kids come to see me. Wanna get drunk with the king. I'm in my rocking chair drunk, drunk already, my kitty on my lap.

"Look," she says, lifting my hand off my kitty, "the same hands."

"A lot of people have the same hands," says Stella.

"The same peasant stock," says girl.

"Napoleon," says I.

I see this girl drooping. She came here to be somebody, but who? Is it Johnnie's kid? Johnnie's kid would be a boy. At the end, everybody lied to me about everything. They said Cody was dead. But how can Cody die? It's Johnnie's kid. She had him and hid him from me.

"I've got to do some research in Mexico," I hear.

"Go ahead," I tell her, "use my name, that'll get you in."

"I gave her my name," I say.

"Excuse me."

"Let's go to that reading."

One thing about Alyce. If you asked her to do something, she did it.

33

It's another one of those little Village bars that got fancy on the inside, brick walls like you'd imagine some hipster's pad if you never knew a hipster, got one room with a little stage in the corner, lights on it, tables all around, then wide doorway opens to barroom where you can sit at bar and still see the stage if you sit near the end by the door. I'm there with Alyce trying to order drink and everybody telling me shh-shh like it's the middle of the love scene of the movie and not some reading in the Village where you should have to yell over the audience to be heard and if you can't, who cares, what makes you think what you've got to say is more important than some drunk's reverie who's paying for his drinks, which is what I tell the bartender but people are turning and yelling at me "shut-up!" Phooey, you shut-up, who's book do you think this is?

"Quiet down," says Alyce.

"Do I remind you of anybody yet?"

"You're starting to."

But then Jan gets on the stage (I should say Mickey, but for reasons which will soon become apparent, also to prevent confusion, I'll say Jan), shows everybody her hands and book *Road Baby*, lots of whooping and hooping, "Quiet down!" I yell, "I can't hear!" but nobody can hear me.

Jan opens book, reads about bumming, trying to be like her Dad who was a famous bum and wrote all about his bumming and made everybody in America want to go out bumming in happy freedom, no responsibility nothing to leave behind because always leaving, though even her Dad, the famous bum, left something behind—her, a remnant bumnant—a reminder that not everything fits in a rucksack (though there was a time she might have fit in there, if he'd chosen to take her she could have fit right in there with his utility knife and army mess kit, a swaddling bumlet), so now, a teen-ager, she goes off in father's footsteps, the backseats of cars, camping out in trainyards, hopping freights, but she's a girl and there are no girl bums, just girl whores, girl sluts, and what to do? she's in old San Luis waiting beside a fire for the Midnight Ghost when she sees a man approaching, and at first he looks small and old, dark skinned, the moon shining silver on his beard, but as he approaches she sees he's a young man in work boots and jeans, slick black hair and white T-shirt rolled up at sleeves, cigarette pack tucked in left shoulder, arms muscular, body and smile of Adonis.

"Where you headed?"

"Anywhere," says she. "How about you?"

"Home," he says. "You know where that is?"

"It's right here."

This is where I want to stop her but it's too late, it's her book. Around me I notice for the first time that there aren't any men in this bar, just women, a whole bar of women, even bartender who now approaches me with face of Mémêre. "Can I get you something? Is there any more I can get you?"

"Don't do it!" I yell to stage. But all the women are yelling, "Do it! Do it!"

"If this is home, then it must be your picture on this key chain," and he shows her his key chain with picture of Virgin of Guadalupe. They're sharing joints and drinks. The air around her is black and cold and the only heat in the world seems to come from him. She opens her shirt to him and gives him her breasts and he takes them in his mouth and unzips her, he tells her that her cunt is the moon. And she's fucked a million bums but never one like him, never one like this bum of San Luis trainyard, the two of them as drunk as stars and as bright as the rails of track reaching into eternity.

"That's my daughter you're fucking!" I yell. "Don't fuck that bastard, he's a ghost! he's death! he's my best friend!" I see it all like horrid vision of devils in Bardo. "My daughter doesn't fuck bums and write about it!" But there are forces whispering in my ear in rapid long speeches advising and warning, suddenly other voices are shouting, the trouble is all the voices are longwinded and talking very fast like Cody at his fastest and zipping too quickly with Jan's voice so that I have to keep up with the meaning though I want to bat it out of my ears—I keep waving at my ears—I'm afraid to close my eyes for all the turmoiled universes I see tilting and expanding suddenly exploding suddenly into my center, faces, yelling mouths, of women, long haired yellers, sudden evil confidences, sudden rat-tat-tats of cerebral committees arguing about "Jack" and talking about him as if he wasn't there—they appear, Johnnie, Alyce, Nin, Laura, Rosie, and Tristessa, Evelyn, Mardou, Billie, and Jan, sad and screaming with calm disdain of me! Stella. Wifey, alive and sad, her face falling from its bones in sadness, "I'm not human!" I scream, "And I'll never be safe anymore!" their faces circling, their faces breasts and wombs—for a moment I see blue heaven and the Virgin's white veil but suddenly a great evil blur like an ink spot spreads over it—the devil's come after me tonight! tonight is the night! but these faces, these angel faces of women now laughing, and suddenly, as clear as anything, I see Mémêre, I see Mémêre up on the cross! her heart is bleeding and she says in sad voice of dying God, "I died for you. We all died for you. Living and dead. We all died."

34

So don't ask why I didn't bus down to Florida and see Stella. I'd said good-bye to her already. I said, "I love you," my last living words, and those are the best last words you can say. Lucky for me she won't read this. But Wifey, if you do, I know you won't believe a word of it. All is vanity. There's nothing new under the sun. That's been said before, too. Go to sleep. Tomorrow's another day. Besides, I love you. So there.

John Clennan Holmes

*Editor's Note

John Clellan Holmes died not long after the reported event and has been unavailable for comment.

Joyce Johnson

Thank you for the read, but sorry to say this isn't for me. It's quite nice at times, but in the end just another Kerouac imitation.

Am I supposed to be Alyce Newman? I suppose I should tell you that I did not attend a reading of Jan Kerouac's work in the Village in 1982, and certainly not with a man I'd just met at an art opening, so needless to say, the man I didn't attend with did not look like an aged Jack Kerouac.

Best of luck finding a publisher.

Jan Kerouac

I don't expect people to understand what it's like to be me. I don't think you have to, to read my work, but it would help. I'm a writer in my own right. I have my own things to say. I'm not just the daughter of Jack Kerouac. Though I am his daughter.

I don't remember if I gave a reading at the Cornelia Street Cafe in 1982, though that's the year I headed off to Boulder to stay with Allen and Peter which is the setting for the beginning of *Trainsong*. Dad's ghost is an important part of that book, as well as *Baby Driver*. There are plenty of sexual interludes in my work. They happen. It's a real part of life, as well as my writing. If it doesn't happen in the way people want it to, well, I'm not living to please anyone, not writing to please everyone. Jack sure didn't.

During one reading in New York back then an older man stood on a bar stool yelling *Hick Alex* or *hickalick, hic calix* maybe, I mean, I hadn't thought of it till just now reading this because as they dragged him out of there he kept yelling "I'm Kerouac! I'm Kerouac!" and we all laughed, but *hic calix* of course is what Dad said at the end of *Vanity*. "'Here's the chalice' and be sure there's wine in it."

35

You take things head on, nobody believes you anyways. Remember, I'm the guy who spent all night with his head in the toilet getting pissed on by drunken sailors. I'm you. You do everything you should do and it comes to nothing. And the only thing I was ever wrong about was that death was some release from all this. Being born so that there can be dying, dying so that there can be being born, the problem is what's in between, the ignorance and pain. That's what. What's in between that? There were moments when Cody lived there, in between the in between, that's why everybody loved him, that's why everybody has to find him (fuck him, be in love with him). So remember when you come back as a ghost you don't come back to haunt but to be haunted. The work of men is football and war and to be fair to women, none of which can be done in a lump if at all. I guess you're never too old or dead to learn something. So buy me a drink and get literary.

36

For example.

Bus to Boston next to some kid from Harvard, plays football.

"Yeah?"

"Yeah, I'm going up for the start of fall practice now."

"What position?"

"Safety."

"Any good?"

"If I was any good I wouldn't be playing for Harvard."

"I played in my day. I played for Columbia."

"They haven't won a game in thirty years."

"Well they won every game I played in. In my day they were the best in the country. Then I left and it was all down hill."

"Some hill."

"You study anything at Harvard?"

"English."

"Oh yeah? Johnson and Pope and Shakespeare and Joyce?"

"I heard of Shakespeare. I don't read much. I only majored in English cuz I didn't know what to major in, and I take mostly writing classes cuz I don't like to read."

"What do you write?"

"You know, stories."

"Any good?"

"I get 'A's."

"I used to write myself."

"Yeah?"

"Yeah, I'm Jack Duluoz. I wrote *Road*."

"I heard of that. I heard it was okay."

"It changed the world."

"You got a copy? If you gave me a copy maybe I could read it sometime."

"I used to carry a copy around but I don't do that anymore."

"Why not?"

"It got published."

"You're funny. My Mom belongs to all those book clubs. You ever get in there?"

"Not recently."

"Maybe if you got in The Book of the Month Club my Mom would send me one. What's your name again?"

"I ain't written in a while. Not since I died."

"You shouldn't talk like that. Attitude is everything. Like money. If you have the right attitude, money will just come to you."

"What's your Dad do, run an airline?"

"How'd you know? My grandfather bought it. But when he inherited his trucking company from his father, he had to build it up almost from scratch. He made Dad go to Harvard before he even let him in the front door. It's hardest on the people from the inside, that's why I'm striking out on my own, taking my graduation money and opening a travel agency or something. You'll notice I'm not flying up to Boston. I even took the train to Chicago once, didn't even get a sleeper. Sat up all night in my seat just to see what it was like. You know some people travel like that all the time. What a trip! I wrote a little story about it and sold it to Dad's airline magazine."

"Want some of this tokay?"

"No downers, thanks. I keep to coke. It's clean. It's white. It's optimistic."

"Helps you keep that good attitude."

"That's right."

"You know how many kids are dying in Mexico for that attitude?"

"They're dying everywhere. I'll die too. Somebody's got to be on the bottom and somebody's got to be on the top. Yin-Yang."

"That ain't what Yin-Yang is about."

"Does it matter?"

37

I guess it does or I wouldn't be writing this last book. And I'm almost at the end so let me get some things straight (because, if you haven't noticed, one thing a little different about this Duluoz is he doesn't do as much explaining—call it the wisdom of hind-sighted death —), I saw myself in that kid; he was at the bottom of the cross and I was Mémêre, crucified and looking down—it's the Virgin up there crucified, not Jesus, Jesus is just some young kid who doesn't know anything, who had it too good up till now—(and the more you explain, you see, the more complicated it gets!) (everything I wrote was for a reason, as if that wasn't reason enough!) (even the parentheses!), forgive me, reader, for I have sinned, it's been thirteen years since my last confession! The writing never stops. Even after you die. Even after your last book.

38

Then it's Lowell in streets of Pawtucketville, Lowell U. looming unchanged over Merrimack River, rain skies and rain streets, old Lowell of rain gray raining, falling down into river day and night, summer winter (and me remembering wet afternoons walking with Wifey in gray days of liquor fast, only way to keep me out of Nikko's Bar, she with me in walks out to old Dracut already even then turning from fields of football baseball memory into plazas, fast food dining, mini-malls, the cleat marks of Duluoz and Iddyboy and whole gang buried under asphalt parking lots where no ball flies—all those windows, you know—Pawtucketville already filling up with new poverties, the Greeks and Russians and French Canucks moving out, the houses and old apartments filling up with Puerto Ricans) and now Vietnamese, Saigoning their oriental ways in streets, satin dragon jacketed, grease haired and corner hanging, the girls waggling toosh to whistles and skittering off embarrassed, their Momma's yelling at the boys buoying street lights with cigarette and switchblade, new races, new bodies, but it's still America, be the same when it's space ports instead of bus stations.

Inside Astro's Sub and Pizza two Puerto Ricans sit at counter smoking Pal Mal's but rest of place is empty with nobody behind bar. They watch me with look of shadowed nuance to stranger—their hang out now, and who am I—but I take stool and wait at bar, ten, fifteen minutes and nothing changes but red white and blue clock on wall over wood paneling unchanged from days of my own counter hanging afternoons, wood paneling peeling now with brown age. "Can't I get something here?" I say to boys. They shrug. Offer of cigarette.

Across University Avenue the brown brick Pawtucketville Social Club of high school afternoon pool shoot, Emil coughing his disapproval in the smoke of ghosts, his cancer written inside, the Club as cold as a Nashua grave, and Mémêre across the street four stories up in that sad air of move to Pawtucketville away from big homes and next door yell to French Canuck housewives, four stories poorer and closer to heaven, from street that old apartment sags sad at building top, crooked window life brown shaded soul visioning shingle drop from walls—here stands Duluoz in space of life small enough to yell stories back and forth across the street, space eating years, years washed away, rain from purple sky raining on Puerto Ricans and Vietnamese—I walk back and forth across the street, my old footsteps on washed avenue, in footsteps of Emil, each step vanishing—nothing dead as memory.

Downtown old mills red brick rise now condos, museums, insurance offices, hi-tech computer brains racing white-shirted in rain streets under intent black umbrella spread, money options spreading in dwindling life options, new American mind ghettos of techno-deductibility, Boston Jr. in downtown Lowell—why here? everything's cheaper—they go home (in BMW commute to Boston, own sail boat), pat wife and kids, watch PBS—probably a show about Irwin Garden on tonight, Hart Crane, me!—I remember that I never voted in an election till I became a drunk.

Here on Market new Lowell Visitor's Center inside old Lowell textile mill (sign says it's part of Lowell National Historical Park, but only thing park-like is kids standing around in kahki uniforms and Mountie hats looking for something to supervise, bear or squirrel, anything, these enlarged photos of canals and interiors of textile mills are a peaceful bunch)—for one thing it gets me out of rain—go up to big desk and talk to young Mountie.

"I'm looking for the grave of a famous writer who lived here born and raised," I tell him.

"Who would that be?"

"Jack Duluoz."

Who he's never heard of so yells across museum to woman Mountie who yells back that I should try Tony in the bookstore, he might know something. Tony is little thin Dago who stands behind counter like vulture, eyes way in his head, too much time in store room, he says, looking for picture books about textile mills, says he commutes to Lowell from Philadelphia, only bookstore job he could get and his wife made him get a job because she was tired of supporting him, he figures with the hotels and commute he's losing about three dollars a day but it gets him out of the house. He's heard of Duluoz.

"Tried to order his books for the store but it got vetoed," he says. "Too many people in town who knew him when he lived here in the sixties said he was nothing but a drunk."

"What's that got to do with his books?"

"Somebody on the Historical Society read one and decided it was perverted. Don't look at me, I think he was the greatest writer in America. The best."

"Me too. I'm looking for his grave."

"Unless you know what you're looking for it's hard to find. Just a flat stone. Take Gorham out—it becomes 3A—take a right into the Edson Cemetery at the gate, there's a caretaker's building on your right, now you're on 3rd Street which you take up to Lincoln Avenue and take a left, take that till you get between 7th and 8th and stop, look for a big grave that says EISENSTRAUT, got bushes on either side, it's in front of that. You have to look down because it's just flat. Says "Ti Jean" on it. Some people find it, you know, kids, there's wine bottles and Benzedrine inhalers, that kind of stuff all around. The wife, Stavroula, is there right on the same little stone with an open death date, and I think that's her brother Sabby, his buddy who got knocked off at Anzio over on the left, though the name on there's Savikacus instead of Savakis. People find it. I hear Irwin Garden was there with Bob Dylan. You familiar with this area?"

"I'll get a cab or something."

"Good luck. You think you're in New York?"

"I want to go up to Centralville and look around."

"Even if you know the addresses, and there's got to be a dozen, his parents moved every other week. Most those places are torn down now I bet. I've been up there. The streets aren't marked, you can't find your way around, the people talk funny. Listen, five, ten years from now this town's going to be sorry because everybody's going to realize that Duluoz was important. There's some people here, you know, who want to build a monument for him, put it over there on the corner of Merrimack and Bridge, right there on the canal across from the mill, big stones with quotes from his books on them.

Nice thing to do for a writer. It'll cost a fortune. Meanwhile they'll let the place he was born in rot. No historical sense."

"They should have done it while he was alive."

"Where have you been living, Argentina? He's lucky he got in print. You have to take the cards you're dealt, even after you're dead."

But you can walk in heart shaped Centralville and if you're lucky it will rain (because rain is tears of memory, tear of sky, brown mind of cloud shrouded Lowell, and little Centralville on the brown snake's river back) (all haunted to this day by liquid of Duluoz)—every house is there—I look from cemetery to 240 Hildreth and see face of young Jackie Duluoz (me) out second story window dream-seeing voids, staring into rain on graves, patter drops on glass and sill the same as drops on stone, old ground of Indians soaking it all in, and below the Moody Street Bridge ghosts riding on rapid crests of mounting surge, from window he shouts and everywhere, the other houses on Phebe and Sarah, up Hildreth (to 320), to West Street, and Beaulieu (where Gerard gave up his little holy life for me, so his saintliness would move my tears for world to ink, his little body carried across the street to St. Louis on black procession of nuns), Jackie, the white dots of ghosts are everywhere, on Burnaby too, one shout and tiny Centralville can hear it all (Father Spike Bisonette still there, leaves St. Jean Baptiste, confessions done, head dipped in rain toward rectory and warm lunch, he, mumbling his dark Latin Offices, sees the shadow souls that ghosts leave trembling on wet pavement in memory rain, lifts head to call of young Duluoz, not a moment has passed in all these years, what is sin, he thinks, but the admission of sin, and that makes all sinners holy) I begin to think that Lowell, Pawtucketville, Centralville live in ghost of me until upon return to 9 Lupine Road and stand in rain in front of house of birth—green shingles drooping from second floor porch held spindling by thin propped two-by-fours, shingles torn from bottom, old white station wagon shambling in drive on left—when young woman appears on upper porch (my porch!), hair brown fallen and eyes of blue, house dress like old wonderment worn like gown of life, she raises one bare arm above her eyes and with other hand touches stomach in that way that pregnant women touch the center of the world, she spots old Duluoz in rain of afternoon, center-streeted old man before his birthplace.

Not wanting to give her alarm I yell, "I lived here once."

"We were fixing it up but we ran out of money," she says to me in French Canuck. In fifty years they still speak French Canuck.

"What's you're name?" says I.

"Beaulieu. Like the street. Louise Beaulieu. My baby, my first baby, is due in March," she says in great motherhood pride of woman girl at center of world, center of life, death, everything on ragged Lowell porch where once, inside, my mother was that young and had such hope of me.

"I lived on Beaulieu, too," I say.

"Well, it's a small town."

"Small world," says I, baffled in circle of birth, death, birth. "Do you know Jack Duluoz?"

"No," she says in that beautiful sad way a woman tells a man *no*. "I don't know if there are any Duluoz left here."

"He was a writer," says I.

"Well, maybe my child will be a writer."

"Don't wish for it," I say, though now it begins to rain hard and young woman ducks inside. I know in my ghostly knowing that she is coming down the stairs, but when she comes out the downstairs door I'm gone, already down beneath the V.F.W. Highway and underneath the Moody Street Bridge. Some children across the way skipping stones at water edge pay no attention to me, either that or because I am a ghost they don't see me. I stand there on the edge ledge. The brown foam fury waters come—brown foam, mud foam—the lonely turrets of houses near the river, the doomed lives of the inhabitants of sorrow in gray afternoon, over the hungry lip of river brown torrential roar, the unforgettable flow, until high above me on the bridge, Dr. Sax, his hollow laugh echoes howling the unspeakable.

I go up to meet him.

And he invites me in to his round black car.

Brown gloves on wheel, drool-eyed, his hat dips. "Been some time," cackles he, and drives across bridge, Pawtucket Street along river, circling down to Lowell High, down Gorham past Nikko's Bar and out to the Edson Cemetery. "Wouldn't want you to lose your way, wa-ha," says Dr. Sax, dripping on his own bones, stops car and points his dipping finger out black sleeve to graves, in that moment change of visage in blue gray light, a silver stubble sprouting on purple skin darkening to red, he points to car ignition where key chain hangs, flag of Mexico and Virgin of Guadalupe, then back again toward graves.

Where out of car and walking I find the flat gray stone in overgrown grass, empty bottle of tokay, broken Benzedrine inhaler, wet copy of *Road*, empty flower dish filled with rain and four brown pennies at bottom in mud.

"TI JEAN"

JOHN L. DULUOZ
MAR. 12, 1922—OCT. 21, 1969
— HE HONORED LIFE —
STAVROULA HIS WIFE
NOV. 11 1918—

And there I am, as dead as I was the day before my mother ever thought of me. The wind shifts and blows the wet pages of *Road* in sluggish drowsy sadness, as heavy as stones. The rain stops. I watch the skies, looking for an evening star. Wind flips *Road* pages on grave until it reaches end. Nobody knows what's going to happen to anybody besides the forlorn rags of growing old. I think of Cody Pomeray. I think of Stavroula, and Mémêre. I think of Cody Pomeray.

And then to the honk of horn I turn back to the graveyard road where young Cody sits at wheel of long black Cadillac, hair combed back, shirt sleeves rolled. "Come on, get in!" he yells. And in car he points to sky that shows the shrouded moon. "There isn't anything else! Just this! NOW! Come on, we're going home!"

About the Author

CHUCK ROSENTHAL is the author of four novels, *Loop's Progress*, *Experiments With Life & Deaf*, *Loop's End* and *Elena of the Stars*. His fiction has appeared in many journals including *The Santa Monica Review* and *The Denver Quarterly*. He is a full professor of English and Creative Writing at Loyola Marymount University.

He lives with poet Gail Wronsky, and their daughter Marlena in Topanga, California.

www.ingramcontent.com/pod-product-compliance
Lightning Source LLC
Chambersburg PA
CBHW020611310726
48979CB00008B/1441/J